Please enjoy.

THE TICK TOCK MAN

R.M. CLARK

Month9Books

To Connor,

Thanks for reading!

Ron Clark

To my mother, Jan. The time is right.

THE TICK TOCK MAN

CHAPTER ONE

Something wasn't right.

I'd planned on sleeping in Thanksgiving morning because, hey, it was Thanksgiving, and that meant no school and no stupid alarm to wake me up. Well, that was the plan.

At precisely eight a.m., the clock sitting a mere two feet from my head wailed.

Thunka thunka thunka thunka.

Stupid clock. That wasn't even a real alarm sound. It was just an invented strange noise to annoy me. I checked the buttons on top. No alarm set and no radio. *Maybe it was a dream?* Just to be sure, I gave the clock a good whack.

All was well. Back to sleep.

Bonka bonka bonka bonka.

Now it was nine o'clock. I sat up and grabbed the clock with every intention of tossing it against the back wall. What a pleasure it would have been to see it smash into a million pieces. I win!

But, this clock was a birthday present from Uncle Artie. He'd said it was "a special clock for a special kid." I didn't like being called "special" because that had a different meaning at school. But it was a cool clock.

Until now. I mean, what kind of noise was that? Certainly not the alarm sound I was used to.

I tried to go back to sleep, but I couldn't help but wonder what crazy not-real-clock noise Uncle Artie's "special" clock would make next. So I got out of bed.

Since it was Thanksgiving, I was not at all surprised to see my mom up and in the kitchen. The turkey was on the counter in a large pan. Her arm was halfway up the turkey's you-know-what. Not what I wanted to see this early in the morning, thank you very much.

"Good morning," Mom said. "You're up early."

"Couldn't sleep." I wanted to mention the special-but-stupid clock that made strange noises at weird times, but she had grabbed another handful of stuffing and stuffed it "up there."

"We'll need a few guest chairs from the basement when

you get a chance. Nana and Papa are coming over, of course. Plus Grandma and Grandpa Boyce. And Uncle Artie too."

"Sure thing, Mom." I was barely awake and she was already asking me to do math. Nobody was coming over for quite a while, so I wouldn't need the, let's see, two-plus-two-plus-one chairs for several hours. I had tons of time.

What better way to spend it than on the couch watching TV? It would probably be the most fun I would have all day, with both sets of grandparents coming over. It was annoying enough that they had different titles: "Nana and Papa" on the Barnes side, "Grandma and Grandpa" on the Boyce side.

Then there was Uncle Artie. He wasn't really an uncle but that's what we always called him. I've also heard him called a "distant cousin," whatever that means. He said his job as an "importer" took him around the world to some pretty exotic places such as Vienna and Timbuktu and South America. No matter what faraway land he went to, he almost always brought us back a clock. We had wooden clocks, metal clocks, cuckoo clocks, and some that were just too odd to describe. Mom would open a package from him and say, "Hey, look. It's a clock. Imagine that."

Each clock came with a wonderful story, so my parents loved to get them for just that reason. Unfortunately, both of them hated having all those clocks, with their constant ticking and chiming, so we kept them stashed away in the spare room upstairs until Uncle Artie came to visit. And since he was on his way, I sat up, knowing what was coming next. In three … two … one.

"CJ! Your Uncle Artie's coming over, so you'll need to set the clocks out." Mom could sure belt it out when she needed to.

I knew the drill. I went to the spare room, pulled the special box out of the closet, and lugged it down the stairs. The crescent moon clock went in the living room, replacing a family portrait, which was fine with me since I looked like a dork in that picture, anyway. There was a special cuckoo clock for the bathroom that was pretty cool. The doors on the upper level opened at the top of the hour, revealing either a boy dancer or girl dancer. I set the correct time and adjusted the weights at the end of a long chain to keep the gears going. Six clocks later, I had completed the task, finishing it off in Dad's basement shop with a clock made from a circular saw blade.

Uncle Artie's favorite saying was, "You can never have too many clocks." On this Thanksgiving Day, it was certainly true, even though I was sure my parents would disagree. Not me. Although I never paid a lot of attention to the clocks, I felt something strange as I took each one from the box and hung it in its rightful spot. The crescent moon clock had two huge eyes, one on the crescent side and the other on the orange side that completed the circle. The eyes were painted on but I swear they followed me as I moved around the room.

I double-checked the time on the cuckoo clock in the bathroom and admired the details in it. The entire clock was a house from a German village, with people dressed in lederhosen on the lower level. Lucky for me it was the top of the hour and the clock chimed, revealing the bird from a door at the top and children dancing in the two small doors just below it. Why hadn't I noticed that before? What awesome detail!

I completed the clock replacement task, storing the non-clock items in the same box and returning it to the spare bedroom. That practically wore me out, so it was back to the couch. The smell from the great stuff Mom was cooking drifted into the room, reminding me I hadn't eaten yet.

"I made you some scrambled eggs." Mom smiled as I entered the kitchen.

"Thanks. I'm starving."

She held out a plate then pulled it back, still smiling. "Just as soon as you bring up the chairs from the basement."

This wasn't fair, but it was the second time she'd asked. The third time would not be as charmed. On my way to the basement, I realized my early morning math was wrong. There were four chairs already in the dining room, so I only needed four more. I could easily get them all in one trip.

I passed Dad's shop right at ten thirty and the heard the blade clock begin to make noise. I turned on the shop light to get a good look and, sure enough, the blade was slowly turning. Clockwise, not surprisingly. Even stranger was that the numbers never moved as the blade turned. A few seconds later, it stopped and went back to normal. Another clock I had never paid much attention to was suddenly freaking out. I hurried back upstairs with two chairs on each arm.

I got my scrambled eggs, finally.

At eleven o'clock, things got even weirder. Dad was up by now, sitting in front of his computer, but that wasn't the weird part. When the hour struck, the crescent moon clock made a strange clicking noise, and those crazy eyes began to wink at me. The painted-on lips between the four and eight went from a Mona Lisa smile to a full-blown grin. I wanted to say something to Mom or Dad, but who would believe me? I went into the bathroom, and the boy and girl dancers in the German village twirled next to each other while the bird stayed home. This was quickly moving into "bizarre" territory. It didn't help when my watch—another gift from Uncle Artie—started chiming a sound I had never heard before. I took it off and stuffed it in my pocket. Problem solved.

I played video games in the back room, trying my best not to look at or listen to any of the suddenly crazy clocks in the house. It was working too, as I finished off another level of Mortal Warfare IV.

"CJ," my mom called. "Please set the table."

"Okay. Just one more level." I sat up as the battle intensified.

"Now would be better. They'll be here in less than an hour to watch the football game."

"I'm on it." I made it past the gatekeeper to complete the level, which allowed me to save my spot in the game.

I grabbed plates and set them out on the table. I took one plate and placed it on the TV tray next to the window. That's where I would sit. The rule was: adults at the big table and kids somewhere else. Sometimes it was a card table when my cousins showed up. Since I was the only kid this year, I would have to settle for a TV tray.

My mom's cell phone rang, and she talked with the phone squeezed against her shoulder as she mixed something in a large bowl. She stopped mid-mix and put the bowl down. "I'm sorry to hear that." Her voice was all serious. She walked out of the room before I could hear any more of it.

I returned to my table-setting duties, grabbing forks, knives, and napkins. The smell of turkey and all the fixings hit me hard as I placed the silverware around the table. Maybe all this work would be worth it. I took another whiff. Maybe.

Mom returned to the kitchen, put the phone down, and stopped stirring.

"Mom, you okay?"

She looked up at me with moist eyes. "Uncle Artie is in the hospital and can't make it for Thanksgiving. He hasn't missed one since your dad and I have been married." She dabbed her eyes with her apron. "Fortunately, it's nothing serious and my parents are heading there right now, so they can't make it until the weekend. I'd better go tell your father. Looks like we'll only need five plates at the table."

No Nana and Papa Barnes? No Uncle Artie? I truly hoped Uncle Artie was okay, but this was my big chance to sit at the head of the table, something I've always wanted to do. The head chair was bigger and had arms, and it felt like a throne. Uncle Artie always got the honors while I was stuck with the TV tray under the window.

I followed Mom out to the garage where Dad was cleaning out the van, getting it ready for our traditional late-afternoon drive. Dad didn't seem too bummed to hear the news about Uncle Artie or his in-laws. He barely looked up as he polished the dashboard. "Yeah, well, sorry to hear about Uncle Artie. He's never down for very long."

The time was right to pounce. "Mom? Dad?"

Dad turned toward me and nearly bumped his head on the visor. "Yes?"

"I wish Uncle Artie was coming today, I really do." I tried my best to act like I was crying. It must have worked because I felt my throat tightening. "His are some tough shoes to fill, but I bet he'd want me to sit in his spot at the head of table.

After all, he gave me this watch for my birthday last year." I pulled it out of my pocket to show them. "And we have the same middle name and everything." I, Carlton James Boyce, was merely guessing at his middle name, hoping neither of my parents knew the truth. "Please? I think I've earned it."

Neither of them thought about it for too long. "It's all yours, kid," Dad said as he leaned on the roof of the van.

"Remember your manners at the table," Mom said. "Uncle Artie would want it that way."

Manners? Oh, please. Uncle Artie smoked a lot, drank a lot, and sometimes swore a lot. In spite of all that, he was my favorite relative. Over the years, besides the watches and clocks, he had given me several toy cars, baseball cards, stuffed animals, and even a five-dollar bill. These gifts were always "our little secret." Plus, he told the greatest stories.

Grandma and Grandpa Boyce arrived a little later, and each gave me a quick hug. It's a terrible thing to say, and I know I'm supposed to love my grandparents without question, but Mom's parents—the "good ones" who actually liked me—weren't coming. If Mom and Dad ever found out I felt that way, I'd be grounded for a month—Dad's typical punishment.

Dad and Grandpa went to the living room to watch the game while the women got the food prepared. I tried to help, but I mostly got in the way.

Everything was ready just before two o'clock, and I grabbed the spot at the head of the table, with Grandma and Grandpa to my right and Mom and Dad to my left. Everyone sat down except Grandpa. He placed his hands on the table and leaned toward my dad.

"I guess this doesn't rate as a special occasion, eh, George?"

"How's that, Pop?" Dad said.

"The Hoffhalder. It's a Thanksgiving tradition, isn't it?"

"You bet it is."

The Hoffhalder was a large mantle clock that sat in the corner of the dining room on what mom called the buffet. The Hoffhalder had been in the family for decades, and Dad would only wind it on special occasions. Uncle Artie always had the honors when he came over.

"I'll do it, Dad," I said.

"Can he handle it?" asked Grandpa. "He's just a child."

I'm right here! I thought. *And I'm not a child anymore. I'm thirteen.*

"Sure he can," Grandma said. "Now, make Uncle Artie proud." She gave me her patented don't-screw-it-up look.

"CJ, just be careful, okay?" Dad said.

"Sure thing." I had seen it wound a thousand times. I took the key from the drawer of the small desk nearby, carefully opened the glass in front, and put the key in the keyhole near the number four. There was another near the number eight. I knew it wound clockwise on the right and counterclockwise on the left.

"Whatever you do, don't overwind it," Grandpa said. He gave anyone who ever got near the clock got the same warning.

I started winding. One turn. Two turns. Then it started to get tight, so I stopped. I placed the key in the left hole and began to turn in the other direction with my left hand. One turn. Two turns. It wasn't getting any tighter. Three turns. That was odd; it usually tightened up by now, but I figured it had just been a while. Four turns and still not tight. I switched to my right hand to finish it up. Five turns. Surely it would start to get tight. Then I heard a faint click, and the key wouldn't move anymore. Uh-oh.

"Everything all right?" Dad asked.

I pulled the key out and put it back in the drawer. "Everything's great." I looked at my watch, and then spun the Hoffhalder's minute hand around until the time was five minutes until two. After closing the glass, I gently moved the large pendulum at the bottom, and the Hoffhalder began to tick. Whew! All was well.

When the Hoffhalder chimed, it made a beautiful sound.

In fact, it seemed to be the only clock sound my family liked. It was a perfect combination of bells and gears and springs working in harmony. We now had three minutes until it would chime on the hour, and everyone at the table waited patiently for the moment to arrive. As the last thirty seconds ticked off, Grandpa nudged Grandma. "Here it comes," he said in a low voice.

The Hoffhalder struck two and began to chime. Once. Then another.

But the second chime lingered way too long and the pendulum began to swing wildly, knocking into the side walls. The chime sound turned into a grinding noise, and the pendulum stopped.

"CJ!" Dad yelled. "What have you done to my clock?"

"He overwound it," Grandpa said while making a turning motion with hand.

"Clearly," said Grandma. "And I'll bet Uncle Artie is rolling over in his grave as we speak."

"Artie's not dead," Mom said. "Just in the hospital."

"I'm sorry, everyone," I said. "I didn't mean to. Honest. It was an accident."

"You're grounded," Dad said.

"For how long?" I asked.

"A month."

"A month? Mom?"

"Don't you think that's a little harsh?" she said.

I looked around the table, and three sets of eyes were on me. Mom reached out and touched my hand. At least someone was on my side.

"That clock's been in the family for four generations," Grandpa said. "Built by the finest clockmaker in Germany."

"And smuggled out on a steamer ship during World War I," Grandma added. "Truly one of a kind. Irreplaceable."

I knew the details by heart, and it just made matters worse. "I'll get it fixed, okay? I have some money saved up."

"Sounds like you snapped the mainspring," Grandpa said, adding a "break in half" motion with his hands.

Grandma leaned over and got as close to me as she could. "It'll never be the same."

"A month," Dad said. He put a finger in my face to make his point. "For breaking my clock."

He continued to glare at me as Mom began to serve the turkey. We ate in near silence.

I had ruined Thanksgiving.

CHAPTER TWO

There's something about my town I forgot to mention. It is without a doubt the most boring place on the face of the earth. All that stuff you hear about small New England towns being quaint and cozy and traditional is all bogus. Sure, our town of Hambleton, population still less than two thousand, has the white church with the tall steeple, just like you see on jigsaw puzzles. Red-brick town hall? Check. Town common with ancient oak trees? Check. Downtown hardware store next to the coffee shop? Check. Nothing of importance ever happens in Hambleton.

We took our after-dinner drive, just like we always did. Five of us piled in the van, with Grandma and Grandpa in the middle seats while Dad drove and Mom took the other front seat (called "shotgun" for some reason). I got the back bench all to myself. I didn't want to be there, but Dad was too ticked off to listen to me. Maybe he figured making me go on this stupid drive was more of a punishment than staying home. He was probably right. I brought along a video game and some ear buds in case the conversation got carried away.

"Beautiful day for a drive," Grandma said. It was still light out as we pulled out of the driveway, but the sun was fading fast. The trees still had some color due to a wet summer, as Dad explained it, so Grandma was right about that.

Grandpa held his watch to his ear, and then tapped on the glass. "Anyone have the time?" He tapped again and played with the winder. "Battery must be shot."

The clock on the radio displayed 4:05. I compared it to my watch, which I had put back on before sitting at the head of the table. The time was frozen at two o'clock. How strange. My watch always worked perfectly. When Uncle Artie gave it to me, he said it was a one-of-a-kind watch that would never need winding. I decided it was best not to tell anyone.

We drove through what we called downtown Hambleton, and only a few people were on the road. It was Thanksgiving, so this was not too surprising. In fact, it was one of the reasons we went for a drive on major holidays. Most people were home, and we usually had the roads to ourselves. Dad and Grandpa liked it that way.

"Take highway eighty-nine north," Grandpa said. He fancied himself as the unofficial navigator for all trips. Mom referred to him as a backseat driver.

We zoomed past the old Baptist church with its white shingles and tall steeple. Classic New England, all the way. On the side of the steeple was a large clock with thick, black hands. The bells rang every Sunday morning just before eleven. Mom told me it was to remind people to get to church.

The time stuck two o'clock, just like my watch. How odd. That clock was always right. We continued up the highway, past a bank on the right with a large sign out front that displayed electronic time and temperature. It was unusually warm at forty-seven degrees and the clock displayed 4:16.

There was another bank on the other side with a large clock on the peak of its roof. The hands were frozen at two o'clock.

Okay, this was officially weird. Electronic clocks were a-okay, but some of the clocks with hands had stopped. All this, combined with the strange things the clocks at our house had done that morning, made me think something was up. After all, they were just clocks. No one else seemed to notice, which didn't surprise me in the least because they were chattering on and on up there.

It didn't take long to get out of Hambleton and into Kingsborough, the next town over. Highway 89 ran straight through the busiest part of town, which was mostly empty. We passed two electronic clocks that both read four twenty. Just ahead were the town library and its old clock with large, metal hands. I pushed against the window to get a good look.

4:20.

So much for my Chicken Little theory. I saw another clock with hands high up on a post in the town park and it was humming along with the correct time. If Uncle Artie were sitting next to me like he was last year, he would have noticed. Of course, he would have leaned over and said with stinky cigarette breath, "The clocks are fine. Quit being such a whiny little pip." That was usually followed by a wink and a playful elbow. He was funny that way.

The adult conversation was turning into an argument, which always happened, so I tuned it out and picked up my video game. Before I got too far, I peeked at my watch, and it was running again. The time was off, so I set it to match the clock on the dashboard.

We went by a few more houses, but it was getting too dark to hit Providence, so we made our way home. The video game helped me block out the arguing and complaining from those up front, so I barely realized we were back in Hambleton. The van made its way past the bank with the electronic clock that displayed 5:05. The bank across the street had clock hands, and I strained to see it in the dim light from the parking lot. It was still stuck at two o'clock. How odd.

The clock on the steeple of the Baptist church was also still at two o'clock. I took a quick peek at my own watch, and it was stopped. It was running when we left town but not when we returned.

Perfect.

It was bad enough I had broken the Hoffhalder, but now I was sure of something else: clocks all over our stupid little town had stopped.

CHAPTER THREE

The first thing I did when we got home was check on the Hoffhalder. It was still in the corner with its pendulum hanging straight down, stuck at two o'clock. A lamp in the corner provided the only light in the room and cast an eerie glow on the old clock. The keyholes near the four and the eight looked more like eyes than I had ever noticed before. And why shouldn't they? It was a clock face, after all. The clock was shaped like a bell curve (I remembered something from math class)—high on top and gently sloped down on each side.

"Returning to the scene of the crime, I see," Grandpa said. He watched me from the corner of the room.

"Leave the boy alone, Warren," Grandma said. "It's bad

enough he broke a valuable, irreplaceable family heirloom. You don't have to make him feel guilty about it."

I tried my best to ignore both of them, and I was so relieved when they finally left the room and went back into the den to watch TV. I hated it when they came over. Both seemed to enjoy picking on me but I never knew why. Maybe because they had several grandkids many years before I came along. The other grandkids had all gone on to be successful grownups and I was still a kid.

Back to the Hoffhalder. I never took a good look at the hands before, so I studied them carefully. They were quite decorative and extremely fancy. The numbers on the face were detailed. Each number was painted in two tones, with a black background and a slightly lighter shade of black down the middle, if that makes any sense. I got right up against the glass—face to face!—and studied the script used to print the company name, Hoffhalder, just under the twelve. I had never paid attention to it before and now I couldn't take my eyes off it.

The next thing I felt was a blast of cold air as everything went dark. I found myself floating just above the ground and shrinking by the second. I was pressed against the glass cover of the Hoffhalder. Then, in an instant, I was inside the clock, right next to the gears and chimes and other clock parts. The clock face absorbed mine, and I couldn't feel my nose or ears. After a few seconds, my vision finally adjusted enough for me to see out into the dining room.

I had become the Hoffhalder! The clock hands were my arms, but I couldn't move them out of the two o'clock position.

What in the name of Uncle Artie was going on?

Okay, CJ, just relax, I thought, as I tried to take in the situation. Apparently I still had a brain, although I couldn't feel anything below my arms. *How had this happened?*

I had some peripheral vision, and I saw Grandpa come into the room. Surely he would help me out of this little jam. I tried to call out, but I had no mouth. Grandpa approached the clock, then walked past it. I tried to synchronize my mind with his by thinking *Help me, Grandpa* over and over. I tried to push that thought from my head to his. A few seconds later, he left the room without even trying to rescue me. My weak attempt at telepathy was a total bust.

I was startled to hear someone calling out to me. It was either Mom or Grandma, but I couldn't tell through the thick walls of the clock. Heck, I was just happy to have some hearing back.

"CJ? CJ, where are you?" Mom entered the room and stood with her hands on her hips. Then she threw up her hands and walked out.

I tried again to respond, but nothing came out.

I knew I couldn't stay here much longer without going completely bananas, so I took a quick inventory of my Hoffhalder self. I could see, I could finally hear a little, and I had these funky clock arms that didn't bend and refused to turn.

I focused on the arms, thinking they were my best chance out of this mess. I found I could push with them. A little. I felt myself separate ever so slightly from the clock face on the first attempt. I focused on my newfound ability and gave another push. This time, my face separated from the clock face, and my own arms returned. I quickly found myself on the outside of the clock, floating back down and returning to my normal size.

What just happened? I thought as I stood on solid ground. My knees finally gave out, and I slid to the ground against cabinet door. *Either the clock just ate me or I had a terrible dream.* I put my hands on my face, satisfied my head was still attached. I looked out between my fingers.

"There you are," Mom said from behind me. "Why didn't you answer me?"

I touched my other important body parts to make sure they had returned in one piece. My voice was still inside the clock, apparently, because I could only reply with a squeak.

"Honestly," she said. "This is no time to turn into a moody teenager."

My voice finally returned. "Sorry. I ... I guess I spaced out for a second."

She gave me a serious Mom look. "It's time to put all these extra chairs back in the basement and all those clocks back in the spare bedroom."

"Sure thing, Mom."

Her look went from serious to concerned as she walked toward me. "Are you okay? You look kind of pale. Stand up." I did, and she examined my face, moving my chin side to side. "And you have some serious dark circles under your eyes. Maybe you should get to bed a little early tonight."

"That's a good idea."

She left me so I could get the chairs folded up. I took two under each arm to bring to the basement, making sure I didn't bang into any furniture on the way out. Before I got there, I passed a mirror in the hallway and nearly dropped the chairs. I took a close look at my face and saw more than just dark circles; I saw the faint outline of the clock hands. My face practically read two o'clock! Someone was coming, so I continued my trek to the basement. After I finished, I sneaked a peek in the same mirror and the imprints of the clock hands were fading away, fortunately.

I went to the spare bedroom and grabbed the box for Uncle Artie's clocks. I replaced them one by one, starting with the crescent moon clock. After the German village cuckoo clock made its way into the box, I noticed something extra strange. All Uncle Artie's clocks were stuck at two o'clock. How come no one else noticed this? That question troubled me as I put the box of clocks in its resting place. It was as if those clocks had something to say but couldn't say it.

When I came back down I gave the Hoffhalder another hard look, this time from the other side of the room. As much as I tried to convince myself this was just a clock, I knew that wasn't the case. It spoke to me, although I couldn't completely understand it.

Things were going from strange to downright weird.

CHAPTER FOUR

Thanksgiving was over (thankfully), and I had the place to myself on Friday since it was a school holiday. I was grounded—I did manage to get it reduced to a week, thanks to Mom—and that meant no TV or video games. I got to keep my phone for emergencies, and my laptop because I told Mom I was in the middle of an important paper, which was true. Well, mostly true. Kind of.

I didn't tell anyone about Uncle Artie's clocks or the clocks I saw on our drive that were all stuck at two o'clock. At least the clocks with hands. Something about that bugged me, so I looked it up on the Internet. Under "types of clocks," I discovered that the term for clocks with hands was analog, and the term for electronic clocks that displayed numbers was digital. Now it made a little more sense. The old-style analog clocks had all stopped, while the more modern digital clocks were okay.

I took inventory of the analog clocks in our house that Uncle Artie hadn't given us, and aside from the Hoffhalder and my watch, there were only three others. One was above the oven, but I don't think it had worked since the 1990s. Another was a small wall clock in the guest bathroom, but apparently no one noticed it had stopped except for me. The final one was the crescent moon clock in the living room. All the other clocks were digital. I still had no idea why they weren't affected.

I kept my distance from them because of what had happened the day before. My face had returned to normal— well, as normal as it could get—but the whole freaky adventure into the clock was still fresh in my mind.

I thought about the rest of the town and wondered if anyone else was concerned that the clocks had all stopped. The local news channel didn't have anything on it. Neither did the local paper. I checked every social media outlet, and nobody mentioned the clocks. Why was it just me?

I walked past the Hoffhalder on the way back to the kitchen and stopped cold. The hands were still stuck at two o'clock, but something was different. The light from the side window hit the clock face just right and it "looked" at me with those keyhole eyes. I didn't want to get sucked inside it again, so I stayed behind a chair. I couldn't look away, and I saw images of other clocks flashing quickly in my brain. Like the Hoffhalder, they spoke to me. I squeezed the sides of my head, hoping they would stop, but they kept coming. Somewhere in the jumble of voices and pictures was an invitation. The clock faces rolled past me, and I didn't know why, but they wanted me to go see them.

I quickly realized we had plenty of clocks in the house for me to visit. I ran upstairs to the spare bedroom and pulled out the box of Uncle Artie's clocks. I removed them and placed them on the floor, each one still stuck at two o'clock. Were these the clocks that wanted me to visit? Apparently not. The voices and images went away. There was no invitation in this room.

I put the clocks away and went back to the Hoffhalder. Once again, the images of clock faces continued, and I could tell they were big faces, like the clocks we had all over town. I just had to see them make sure I wasn't imagining this whole crazy story.

Unfortunately, I was grounded, so that put a major damper on my plans. Mom wasn't due home until just after noon, so I had almost two hours. Plenty of time. She would never know.

I texted my friend Brad to see if he was up for a bike ride. I met him at his house a few blocks away. Brad rode a bike that was about three sizes too small, like a clown bike.

"Where we heading?" he asked. It was late November, but Brad was wearing shorts and a T-shirt. He never seemed cold, even though he was skinny like me. I played it safe and wore jeans and a sweatshirt.

"Just into town. There's something I want to see."

Brad was never one to argue. In fact, he'd do almost anything to get out of the house. He nodded and sped up the road ahead of me in the general direction of town. I caught up a block later.

We arrived at the old Baptist church after ten minutes of heavy pedaling. I was somewhat relieved to see the clock still stuck at two o'clock. At least I hadn't imagined it. We pulled up near a fire hydrant on the nearest corner and stopped.

"Why are we stopping? It's some stupid old church."

"Look at the clock."

"Yeah? What about it?"

"See anything unusual?"

He put a hand above his eyes to block the sun. "It's just a clock. Why do we care about a stupid old church and its stupid old clock?"

I swear, sometimes he's as dense as a doorknob. I had my phone with me. It was a pretty cheap one, but at least it kept good time. I held it out as I cleared my throat. "According to my phone, it's ten thirty-three. Now does the clock look unusual?"

Brad made an exaggerated motion with his arm. He looked at his watch, then the clock, then back to his watch. Suddenly, his eyebrows furrowed, and he turned all serious. "That's awesome, dude. The time is ten thirty-three—wait, ten thirty-four— and yet the big clock on the church says ten thirty-six. Thanks for sharing that with me. I guess God's running a little fast, today."

The church clock was clearly stuck at two o'clock, just as plain as day. "Uh, Brad. Look again. It's stuck on two o'clock."

"I learned how to tell time in the first grade. Little hand's just past the ten. Big hand's on the six. That's not two o'clock in any time zone." He awkwardly struck a pose with his arms in the ten and six position. It wasn't pretty. He made a terrible clock.

"Funny." I started back up the road. "But there's something else I want to show you."

The good thing about living in a small town is that it didn't take long to get anywhere important. We kept heading north and soon came to the two banks with the two different types of clocks I'd noticed the day before.

"Check out the two bank clocks. Now do you see what I mean?" The bank on the right had a working digital clock, while the one on the left was stuck at two o'clock.

"I do get it now."

Finally. "Pretty strange, huh?"

He sarcastically put his hand to his chin as he looked from one clock to the other. "Yep. It's strange how one clock can show ten forty-one with moving hands and the other displays ten forty-one without them. Two clocks. One time. Simply amazing."

Not again! The clock on the left absolutely showed two o'clock. No way was I imagining it. My plan was off to a horrible start, so I improvised and took out my watch from my front jeans pocket. "I was wearing this watch when I overwound and broke my parents' Hoffhalder, an old German clock. Every clock in town with a face stopped at that exact time." I gave him a quick summary of our post-Thanksgiving car ride and what I saw. Then I showed him my watch. "See, stuck at two o'clock, thanks to me."

Brad took the watch Uncle Artie gave me and looked at it for a few seconds before handing it back. "I don't get the joke. You say the clocks have stopped. You say you broke your parents' Hasselhoff."

"Hoffhalder."

"Whatever. I look at the same clocks and see the right time. Your watch is a little slow, but we're not in a time warp or anything like that. This is boring, and I have better things to do." He sped off before I could say anything. "I hope your Hasselhoff gets better!" he yelled as he turned the next corner.

Hoffhalder. I wanted to scream the name back to him, but he was gone.

I went back the way we came, pedaling slowly with my head hung low. Whatever was happening was happening to me and me alone. I took another look at my watch. It was definitely, no doubt about it, stopped at two o'clock on the nose. Why couldn't Brad see it?

Before I knew it, I had arrived back at the old Baptist church. I wanted to make sure my eyes weren't completely deceiving me, so I rode my bike to the front of the church, where the clock loomed large about halfway up the steeple.

Two o'clock. No matter how I looked at it, the results were the same. The big question remained: why was I the only one who could see it? Okay, I hadn't asked everyone in town, but Brad couldn't see it was broken, and that was good enough for me. I put my hand up to block out the sun as I looked up at the clock face. It had Roman numerals instead of numbers, which gave it a religious look for some reason.

The hands were straight and plain, except for a thin gold thread running down the middle of each one. If I moved side to side, the gold caught the sun just right.

Like the Hoffhalder before, I found myself strangely attracted to the big clock. It called to me, so I put my hands on the white shingles and closed my eyes. I felt an odd vibration and heard a faint hum.

Then my watch started going crazy. The big hand began spinning, moving past each hour in just a few seconds. I kept my left hand against the shingles and waited. Somehow, I knew what to do. The vibration got stronger. The humming got louder. The watch came back around to two o'clock, and I pulled the knob to make it stop.

Then everything went dark.

CHAPTER FIVE

I knew I was inside the clock, but for some reason, I wasn't scared. My vision returned, and I found myself near the clockworks, dangerously close to a large, turning gear. There was another, larger gear just above my head. To my left I could see the hands and the numbers of one face, and to my right the hands and numbers of the other. The steeple was covered in white shingles, but I could see through them. *How could that be?*

When the Hoffhalder grabbed me, I was a kid squeezed into a house clock, looking out a tiny face. But these clock faces were twenty feet tall. I could also hear the sounds of the town—cars driving by, the distant power plant, kids playing in the nearby playground—but I could also hear other voices coming from some other place. They weren't behind me or below me; the voices were *inside* me. It was all strange, and I was beginning to get used to it.

From just behind the large Roman numeral V I could see Brad pedaling away on his bike a few blocks over. Man, if he knew where I was, he'd be so jealous. I yelled to him, but nothing came out. It's not like he would've heard me anyway. I moved freely from clock face to clock face, ducking gears and viewing town from my high vantage point. As I kept at it, my hearing became more focused and the voices in my head became clearer. I stopped long enough to make out one of the voices.

Who are you?

"My name is CJ," I answered. It was more a thought than an outright statement. I was ready to repeat it, but the voices stopped, and all I could hear was the wind and the occasional noise from the street below.

Which side are you on?

Those five words were as clear as day, so I took a good look around. There was more to this place than just a clock in a steeple. I hadn't noticed that I was walking on a narrow catwalk complete with handrails. I took a few steps and came to the other side of the clockworks, where the catwalk met the side of the steeple. The steeple was solid from the outside—that much I was sure of—but I could see the catwalk stretching out beyond it. This place was getting stranger by the minute.

"Who are you?" I heard once again. It was a nice voice.

I turned. Standing on the other side of the catwalk was a small girl in a white dress. The dress was narrow at the top and flared out quite a bit at the bottom, giving it an unusual cone shape.

"I'm CJ. Who are you?"

"My name is Fuzee."

Fuzee? Now that was a new one.

"Which side are you on?" she asked. I detected a slight accent, perhaps German.

I used the railing to keep steady on the narrow catwalk. Fuzee seemed to have no problem as she stood perfectly still with her arms folded.

"I'm not on any side," I said. "I just got here."

She looked me over from head to toe as she moved a few steps closer. "Then who do represent?"

Represent? This girl was speaking in riddles. I repeated the question to myself several times and it came to me with a little help from some of the strange voices. "I represent the ... Hoffhalder. It has been in our family for many years."

Her expression changed to a smile, which let me know I

had said the right thing. She came closer, and I got a good look at her face. It was round and pretty, and framed by curly brown hair. Her nose and mouth were normal enough, and her skin was shiny, as if she were painted with flesh-colored paint. And those eyes. They were sort of gray and extremely big, like cartoon eyes. Was she human? She sure sounded like a real girl.

She held out her hand but turned quickly before I could take it. I noticed it was a real hand with five fingers. Then both of her hands went to the sides of her head like she was listening for something.

"What is it?" I asked.

She ignored me and continued to listen. When she turned to me, her expression was serious. "One of the Verge is coming this way. You shouldn't stay here, CJ of the Hoffhalder. Be well."

She sped past me in a blur and disappeared down the catwalk. I heard a grinding noise coming from the other end of the catwalk, very similar to the one the Hoffhalder made when I overwound it. I was a sitting duck and had no intention of meeting the Verge, whoever or whatever they were. Even the name gave me the creeps. I made my way past the cogwheels and gears until I came to a spot just next to the face. My watch appeared to be my ticket out, so I pushed the timing knob, and the minute hand began to spin quickly. My left hand touched the cold wall as the grinding got louder. With a click I pulled the knob at precisely two o'clock, and I was back outside with my hands against the white shingle. Daylight.

I was still in tune with the big clock and I could feel a presence on the catwalk I had just left.

Which side are you on? The voice was deep and low and definitely not Fuzee's. I took my hands off the clock tower and stepped away. The voices stopped.

My bike was just where I left it, so I got on it and pedaled away. It would have been easy just to head home and forget any of this had happened. But I couldn't forget. Quickly, the images of Fuzee and the Hoffhalder flashed in my head. The Verge were there too. I could *feel* them. Something strange was going on that other world, and it tore right through me. I saw Fuzee's face again, and I didn't want to forget. In fact, I was all in. Instead of turning right to go home, I took a left. I knew I could be in more trouble, but there was another big clock I just had to visit.

CHAPTER SIX

The wind was whipping pretty fast by the time I reached the northern part of town and the small strip mall on the left side of the road. Disconnected from the rest of the mall was our branch of the Great Northern Bank. Unlike the old Baptist church, the bank was new, although it was made to look like it had been around for decades. The analog clock was above the drive-through window and still stuck at two o'clock.

I parked my bike and put the kickstand down. Looking up, I studied the clock face to try to figure a way "into" it. Last time I just let the voices from the clock guide me there. Would it work again? This was going to be difficult because there were no lower walls on the clock tower, so no obvious place to enter without getting run over by a Volvo.

A quick trip to the back of the bank didn't help. Even if I could find an entry point, the place was just too crowded to try anything. I stopped for a moment and closed my eyes. I could hear the mysterious voices in the clocks. Just as I thought—more people were in there. The voices were low and muffled. Images began to flash in my head. I saw other clocks. Other portals. The town was loaded with them.

I ran back to my bike and rode to the next closest clock, based on what the voices in my head were saying. It was the one at the old train depot a few blocks away. Even though the train didn't come through our town anymore, the depot was still a historic spot. High up on the red brick tower was the depot clock, stuck at two o'clock. I was somehow connected to the clocks, and I needed to write down what I knew before I forgot. I never carried a pen, pencil, or paper with me, so I looked around the depot. There was an information booth with some pamphlets about the depot and its history. Near the top, someone left a small pencil, like ones they give you at a mini-golf course. One of the pamphlets was mostly blank on the back. I grabbed it and began to draw the images as they came to me. I was pretty good with a map, so I made a crude drawing of the town's main streets and filled in the clocks. The old Baptist church. Great Northern Bank. The train depot. Ridley Park. The high school. The Methodist church on the other side of town. I drew them until the images stopped; then I admired my handiwork. I couldn't believe it at first, but I trusted my version of the town layout. Each clock was represented by a small square on the map.

Twelve clocks. Twelve squares.

They were the main clocks—the big public ones—and they formed a near-perfect clock face. But that wasn't the freakiest part. I looked up at the clock above the train depot. Instead of numbers, it had twelve black squares. I held my makeshift map at arm's length and positioned it next to the clock face. My drawing matched it perfectly. "Uncanny," as Uncle Artie would say. Actually, he would always put a swear word in front of uncanny, but I know what he meant.

I put the map in my pocket and set out to see the other clocks. I knew they would all be stuck at two, just like the ones I had already seen, but I had to see them and, more importantly, feel them. I pedaled hard toward Ridley Park and found the sidewalk that led directly to the center of the park, where the clock sat on top of a tall, metal pole. The clock had four faces, making it visible from any direction. All four displayed the same time.

I could hear the inhabitants inside as I leaned against the pole. The sound was fuzzy and hard to hear due to traffic and people in the park. Another noise interrupted them all. It was my stomach growling. I took out my cell phone and checked the digital display for the real time. It was nearly eleven thirty. If I wasn't back before my mom got home from work, I was in some serious trouble.

I pedaled at top speed out of the park and made a beeline home. The quickest way was to cut across the high school grounds, so I banked right and gunned it again. As I zoomed along the sidewalk in front of the school, I could hear the voices coming from the big clock above the entrance.

Which side are you on?

Once again, it wasn't Fuzee's voice. That much I knew. It was gone a few seconds later as I tore past the back parking lot and through a small patch of woods.

From a block away I could see that I was in big trouble. Mom's car was in the driveway. I skidded to halt and leaned against a mailbox to consider my options. *What was she doing home?* My strategy session didn't last long because Mom came outside and stood on the front walkway. It only took a quick glance for her to spot me, so I pedaled home.

"You do know what 'grounded' means, right?" she said.

I got off my bike. "Sorry, Mom, it's just that—"

"Save it!" Her hand was out and nearly in my face. I knew from experience that this was no time to argue. "Get back in the house."

I put my bike in the garage and went in through the side door. It was barely shut before she was all over me.

"It took me two hours last night to convince your father that a month was too long to be grounded. I went to bat for you, and this is how you repay me."

"But I was just—"

She quickly cocked her head sideways, which was her way of saying "Zip it." So I did.

"I came home to pick up some files off my laptop. We're severely short-staffed today, so I have to go back. Can I trust you to be *grounded* for the next few hours?"

"I'm pretty sure I can handle that."

"Is that a yes?"

"Yes."

"Good." She handed me a folded slip of paper. "I have a list of chores for you to do. If they are done when I come home, I may just forget to tell your father you left the house."

"Thanks, Mom."

"I have to go." She left without a goodbye. Not that I deserved one.

I waited until she drove away then looked at the list. It was all easy stuff, so I guess she wasn't too mad. I figured I may as well get the first item—empty the dishwasher—out of the way, so I went straight to the kitchen. I made it as far as the dining room before I realized something was terribly wrong.

The Hoffhalder was gone.

CHAPTER SEVEN

I was in bigger trouble. Not only had I broken the precious family clock, but now someone had stolen it right out from under our roof. I checked the table where the Hoffhalder sat for years, and all that remained was a clean rectangle on the dusty table. Dad was sure to blame me. He would find out I left the house when I was grounded and that when I was gone someone had come in and snatched it up. Make that mega-trouble. Giga-trouble.

I tried to come up with different scenarios for how it may have disappeared. Mom came home but apparently never went into the dining room. It's off to the side, so why would she? I went from room to room and checked all the other doors and windows. They were all locked, so I was sure no one had broken in. Maybe Dad took it with him so he could drop it off to get fixed? I honestly wanted that one to work, but the clock was here in plain sight long after everyone else had left. If it was stolen, I'd have to call my parents and the police.

I'll be grounded for two months.

I get hungry when I worry, so I grabbed some leftover turkey and warmed it up. I ate as I considered my next move. There was a lot of information to process in a short time. I sat at my computer and thought it over. First, all the big analog clocks had frozen in time, but only I was aware of it, or so it seemed. If that wasn't enough, there appeared to be an alternate world inside the clocks where nice people like Fuzee and bad, well, whatever they were, like the Verge existed. I looked up those names on my computer and saw that "fuzee" and "verge" are clock parts. That didn't surprise me one bit. Also, the town clocks were spread out in the shape of a clock face.

I hadn't forgotten that the Hoffhalder was gone. That one made no sense, and I couldn't make a connection.

The two-tone gong of the front doorbell interrupted my thought process. I wasn't expecting anyone, and my friends knew to call or text before coming over. I peeked through the small window next to the door, but the visitor had his back turned. I was taught never to answer the door to a stranger, but a "little voice" told me it was safe. I hesitated, then unlocked and opened the door.

"Hello."

It was Uncle Artie. He was a lot paler than I remembered as he stood there in a black trench coat and sunglasses. I tried to speak, but I could only get as far as blubbering.

"Aren't you going to let me in?" he asked.

Finally, a voice. "S-sure." I swung the door open all the way and stepped aside. He started past me, then stopped and gave me a huge hug.

"Great to see you again, Carlton."

"You too, Uncle Artie." He was the only person who called me Carlton. It seemed okay coming from him.

He let go and brushed past me quickly. For a guy who was seventy or so, he sure had a spring in his step. "Anyone else home?" he said, looking nervously around the room.

"No, I—"

"Good. Listen, we don't have much time. Something strange has happened. We have to act quickly." He typically spoke in short sentences for some reason.

"I thought you were, you know, sick. Mom said you were in the hospital."

"I was. Chest pains turned out to be gas. Got out this

morning. Now I'm here. Everything's weird. Town's gone crazy."

It was the longest I had ever heard him go without swearing. Maybe he did it because of me. Then again, it was hard to tell. There was one thing I knew more than anything: I needed answers.

"Where's the Hoffhalder, Uncle Artie? You took it, didn't you?"

He looked right at me for the first time since he arrived. "I did. Had to, though. Town's gone crazy."

He was starting to repeat himself, so I took the opportunity to find out more about the clock world I visited earlier. "What is the Verge, Uncle Artie? I've been told to avoid them."

Hearing that seemed to cause him pain. He tried to hide it but I could tell. "Who told you about the Verge?"

"Fuzee. I met her inside the big clock—"

He touched my arm. "Let me tell you something. Don't mess with the Verge, okay? If they go east, you go west. They enter, you leave. Got it?"

"Yeah, but *who* are they?"

"Can't tell ya the whole story. Just, please, promise me one thing. You'll not mess with them, okay?"

"Well, I guess—"

He grabbed me by the shoulders and gave me a hard shake. "Okay?"

"Sure. Fine. Okay, Uncle Artie, I promise. Geez, I just want to know what's going on, that's all."

Uncle Artie nodded slowly and put his right hand on my shoulder. "All right, then. I'll tell you what I know. First, you got any booze in this place?"

Now that was the Uncle Artie I knew and loved. Well, maybe liked a little. "I think there's a beer in the fridge. Dad sometimes—"

"I'll take it. Tell you what. You get me the beer, and I'm gonna head outside for a smoke. You gather up every timepiece in the house, okay? Gather 'em up and put 'em on the living room floor. Anything analog. Watches, cuckoo clocks, alarms. Get 'em all. Got that?"

"Yeah, sure." I got his beer from the refrigerator, and he snatched it quickly from my hand.

"I know you don't have any of the clocks I sent you hung up. Your mom probably made you put them away when she heard I wasn't coming. Am I right?"

"Um … "

"Doesn't matter. Just bring 'em in, and the others too." He turned and headed out the front door.

I quickly got all his clocks, but I had to think about

where the others were. I went from room to room looking for analog clocks. I found a small wall clock in the guest bathroom. It was a cheap clock that spelled out BATH with the clock movement in the bottom of the B. The clock on the oven popped out with a little push from the back, and I almost dropped it on the floor. I remembered I hadn't put the saw-blade clock away, so I grabbed it from the shop. Every one of the clocks—even the ones that hadn't worked in a long time—read the same time: two o'clock. I added the saw blade to the pile just as Uncle Artie returned. He was empty-handed, so who knows what happened to that beer can and the cigarette butt.

"That's all of them, Uncle Artie. Every clock is accounted for." I was proud of my clock pile and swept my hand across it to prove it.

"No. There are more."

"But, I—"

"I'm telling you, there are more clocks in this da—in this house." He almost swore but caught himself. I guess he had a hard time swearing around a kid. "I can feel it."

"What do you mean you can feel it?"

"Listen, I've been—" He stopped and picked up the bath clock and examined it. "I mean, I'll explain later. There's another watch in your parents' room. Probably in a drawer somewhere." He closed his eyes and scrunched his face. "And check the laundry room. I think there's one in the back corner. Now go." He shooed me with a wave of the clock he still held in his hand.

I went upstairs to my parents' room and looked around for the missing watch. It felt creepy and downright strange to be going through their stuff, but this seemed important. I tried to think where an old watch might be stashed, and a familiar feeling came over me. The clocks spoke to me. They told me the nightstand on Dad's side would the most logical place. It was there, all right, behind a pile of handkerchiefs.

I stopped at the top of the stairs and looked down at Uncle Artie. He was arranging the timepieces in a circle on the floor. I descended the stairs and went straight to the laundry room. The old clock was right where he said it would be. Uncle Artie knew, the same way I knew.

When I returned to the living room, his circle was nearly complete. I interrupted his swearing and handed him the final two clocks. The circle was about six feet in diameter.

"We'll need some batteries. AA, more than likely."

I barely heard him. All I could focus on was the crazy circle of clocks and watches. "What are you doing, Uncle Artie?"

"You'll see. Just get the f—I mean, just get the batteries."

Once again he left me confused and angry as I went hunting for batteries. I wanted to tell him it was okay to swear in front of me. I wasn't a kid anymore. Fortunately for him, we have one of those "everything" drawers in our kitchen, and I found a four-pack of AA batteries in the back. I opened the pack and grabbed all four, then peeked cautiously around the corner to the living room. Uncle Artie was mumbling something as he adjusted the timepieces.

"Here you go." I got close to his circle. It looked like some sort of clock voodoo ritual.

"The bath clock needs new batteries. All the others need winding or have broken mechanisms. I'll wind; you put in the batteries."

He picked up a pocket watch and began to twist the top. I flipped over the bath clock and put in a fresh AA. The hands remained stuck at two o'clock. Somehow, I had a feeling something weird was going to happen, but I didn't dare say a word.

Uncle Artie made a final adjustment to the position of the saw-blade clock and stepped back in the circle. "You have that watch I gave you last year, right?"

I pulled it from my pocket and showed him. "Right here."

"Good. Now hold onto it. I'm only going to show you this once, you little pip. Step inside the circle."

I took a shaky step as I held the watch in my left hand. I switched it my right to keep from shaking. Unlike before, the watch hands were set to the correct time.

"This will help explain what's going on. What we have here is called an isochronal circle." He had another watch in his hand, and he made some small adjustments to it. "There should be just enough mainspring action in these babies to get where we want to go."

"And where do we want to go?"

He looked up, and I braced for a mean comment. But he just smiled. And winked! "You'll see. I want you to take that watch and set it to two o'clock. Press the timing knob when you're done. Oh, and be ready to stop it when I say so."

I did as he said and set the time with a *click*. The clocks and watches began to rise, some higher than others, until they were three feet or so off the carpet. Uncle Artie set his watch, and the clocks began to swirl around us, slowly at first. The saw blade glistened as it spun, and the circle was filled with what looked like sparks or small stars. Faster and faster the clocks spun around us. It was better than the Fourth of July. It was awesome!

"Stop, Carlton."

I barely heard him as the timepieces began spinning slower.

"I said stop, you little pip!" He reached over and pulled

up on the time knob of my watch. The show was over as the clocks dropped back to the carpet.

"That was amazing," I said. "What does it mean?"

"It means we have plenty of mainspring action. We can get there from here."

I almost dreaded asking, but I had to know. I moved out of the circle so I was not in his way. "So where is 'there'?"

"Furtwangen."

"What kind of place is that?"

"You've already seen a small part of it."

"The clock world? So that's what they call it." I immediately thought of Fuzee and hoped I'd see her again.

He made some slight adjustments to the placement of bigger clocks as I watched from the ottoman. "What time are your parents coming home?"

"Both are working all day. Why?"

"Get back in the isochronal circle. It's ready to go." He made a final adjustment to his watch.

"One problem, Uncle Artie. I'm grounded for breaking the Hoffhalder. Mom and Dad will kill me if I go anywhere."

"Don't worry about your parents, kid. I'll take care of 'em." He put his hand out. "Trust me."

I joined him in the circle and set the time on my watch as before.

"Ready?" he asked as he pressed the time knob. The timepieces rose.

"Ready."

With a *click* of my watch, the timepieces once again began to swirl. Faster and faster they buzzed around us, sparks lighting the room. Uncle Artie pulled me close to his side and held on.

We set our watches at the same time, and everything went dark.

CHAPTER EIGHT

It was called Furtwangen, but this was the clock world, no doubt about it. The second we left our living room, we were somehow transported to a place overlooking Ripley Park in the middle of town. I could tell we were inside the large, four-sided clock in the park. I grabbed the handrail to steady myself, then realized I didn't need it. A layer of misty fog hung just below the catwalk, occasionally making its way up to the rails. It didn't bother me, and I was getting pretty good at moving around in Furtwangen.

Uncle Artie stayed a step ahead of me the entire time as we made our way down the catwalk. He hadn't kept me as informed as I would've liked during his visit, so I figured it was a good time to get caught up.

"Uncle Artie, where are we going?"

We ducked under a giant gear, then he stopped and leaned against the rail.

"Okay. Time for some answers. First of all, I ain't your uncle, so knock off the Uncle Artie stuff."

"I knew that. Mom says you're a distant relative."

"That may be true, but I'm not entirely sure. I'm an only child. I'm not anyone's uncle."

I hadn't noticed that somewhere along the way he'd ditched the black overcoat and now had on a black, short-sleeved shirt. He was much more muscular than I thought.

"So what can I call you?"

He put his ripped arms out and spread them wide. "In this world, I'm known as Ratchet Dog. But most people call me Ratchet. By the way, has anyone ever mentioned why you were named Carlton?"

"No. I always assumed my parents just liked the name."

"Truth is, I convinced them to name you Carlton. That name is huge in the world of English clockmaking, nearly rivaling the Germans. It's a classy name. For a classy kid."

Now that I knew about my name, I focused on his. A ratchet dog was another clock part I read about online. The ratchet dog keeps the mainspring working. But how did he get involved in all this? He did say it was time for answers, so

I would just have to press on and ask more questions. "Why is this place called Furtwangen? It sounds German."

We came to a narrow passage and had to stoop several times while we maneuvered around a long cog arm. I was getting to know my clock parts pretty well.

"Take everything you know about your town and toss it out the window. None of it's accurate."

"What do you mean?"

"This town is called Hambleton, right? Nice name for a town. Founded by a couple of fellows from another Hambleton. The one back in jolly ol' England, right? That's pretty much how all the towns are named around here."

"That's what our fifth grade teacher told us." The catwalk took a sharp left turn, so I held onto the handrails as we maneuvered.

"Truth is, this town was first settled by a couple of German clockmakers. They came from Furtwangen in the Black Forest. Got here years before those other town founders arrived. No one could pronounce the crazy name. Too German. So they let the Hambleton folks have it. Bet your teacher never mentioned that tidbit."

Nope, she hadn't. If it was true. I still wasn't sure if Uncle Artie—I mean Ratchet—was a reliable source.

"Just so you know, there's a name for those of us who can

go between worlds. We're called spandrels. Have you heard that before?"

"No." It sounded like a breed of dog, but I didn't mention it.

"Think of it this way. Picture a large square. Then picture the biggest circle you can fit in that square. You got that?"

"Sure." It was more math, but I was following.

"Everything outside the square is your parents' world, your town. Everything inside the circle is Furtwangen. In architecture, that weird space between the corners of the square and the arch of the circle is called spandrel. That's what we are. Kind of in, kind of out." He swept his hand from one side to the other. "The best of both worlds if you think about it."

I did think about being a spandrel. Cool name.

There were a few others ahead of us on the catwalk. They were small, spring-like folks with tiny heads and big eyes who quickly moved down a side path as we passed. Other odd-looking characters stood on the path and made no attempt to move as we squeezed by them. Some of them looked almost human.

Then the smell hit me. It was a sour, sickly smell I vaguely remembered from my first trip to Furtwangen. Ratchet's nose began to twitch, so I knew he smelled it too. The smell was followed by a low grinding noise.

"This way," Ratchet said. "Behind the gong rods." We slipped off the path and hid behind a series of long brass tubes. I had seen these in many clocks. They were also called chimes. We tucked in tightly, completely out of view from anyone on the catwalk.

The smell got stronger as the odd noises got closer. In a flash, they were by us.

The Verge.

"They don't care about us," Ratchet said. "We're fairly insignificant."

Sure, he said it with confidence, but his right hand shook as he steadied it against the tallest gong rod. I figured it was best not to mention it.

"You were saying?" I said, trying to get him back on the topic at hand.

"Ah, yes. Furtwangen." We both looked up and down the catwalk; then we continued on our journey. "Those two clockmakers had a bit of a falling out. They both stayed in town. Both opened clock shops. Feuding German clockmakers is not in the recipe for a quiet New England town. They were shunned by the locals. They declared a truce. Later decided the best way to remain vital to the town was behind the scenes. They created two factions: Kinzig and Murg. The north and the south. They take care of the clocks.

They make sure the hands keep running. They make sure the gongs keep chiming. That's what the people want. Get it?"

"I think so." In reality, I had no idea what he was talking about. Feuding clockmakers? Kinzig and Murg? A town divided? This was going to be a slow process, I could tell. Still, I was glad to be part of this journey. "So where's the Hoffhalder?"

He stopped in mid-stride, and I nearly bumped into him. "It's safe. Please don't ask me about the Hoffhalder again. It's better if you don't know." He glared at me for a few seconds, then turned and walked on.

The path was circular and I more or less figured out that we were traveling counterclockwise between all the town clocks. The "why" part of that equation had yet to be answered, but the day was still young.

Ahead of us was something unexpected: a door. It was tall and metal with no doorknob or keyhole. Just a door. Fortunately, the path took a sharp left around it.

"What's that?" I asked.

"Behind that door is the mainspring. The mainspring is the key component to any clock. You know the feeling you get when you wind a clock? It gets tighter and tighter as you go, right? That's the mainspring in action. Chimes and cuckoos and all that are nice. Without a mainspring, though, you got nothin'. You get what I'm saying?"

I got it all right. When I overwound the Hoffhalder, I messed up the mainspring. I messed up everything, apparently.

As we went around this mainspring, I noticed something odd. There were no walls protecting it, yet I couldn't see it. We took a right turn and were back on track, the mainspring still hidden from view by some unknown force.

Our trek continued as we ventured from clock to clock. It didn't take long to get to the train depot clock. Ratchet was tiring and he grabbed both handrails to steady himself. He had been too far ahead for me to get any answers, so maybe now would be a good time.

"How much farther, Ratchet?"

"We get off here at the depot." He took a cloth from his pocket and wiped his forehead.

"Then what?"

"Then it's off the Furtwangen."

"I thought we were in Furtwangen."

"Well, not exactly. This circular area is called the Sequence. We'll head along that path—" he pointed with a boney finger "—and that will take us into Furtwangen. But before we go, I need you to remember something."

"Sure, Ratchet. You name it."

He grabbed me by the shoulders, just like he did earlier in my house. "Two things you need to know about life in

Furtwangen: one, every clock has a face, and behind every face, something is ticking. Do you know what I'm saying?"

I tried my best to understand what he was saying, but I still couldn't quite figure out the whole clock/human side of all this. I hated to do it, but I told him a lie. "Sure, Ratchet. I get it."

He released my shoulders but continued to look at me without blinking. Did he know I was lying? I was sure I could figure out this stuff eventually. I gave him my most serious look right back. Finally, he nodded ever so slightly and patted my arm. "Okay, you little pip. Let's get moving."

He started to turn, but this time, I grabbed his shoulder. "You said there were two things. What's the other?"

"Two: be careful who you trust."

With that, we headed down the catwalk toward Furtwangen. A large pendulum swung in front of us, but it was easy enough to maneuver around. The mist was less noticeable as we moved inward, away from the Sequence (another cool clock-part name, by the way).

The foul smell filled my nostrils. It was gag-worthy and made me stop. Next thing I knew, there was a grinding sound, and something struck me. I was flat on the catwalk after my head banged a rail. Ratchet was pulled the other way toward the light. It was the Verge. I just knew it.

"Carlton! Run! Go back to the way we came!" Two of them grabbed him by the arms. They had heads shaped like gears that could spin around quickly, even though their giant eyes never moved. They wore black overalls and black shoes. Ratchet backhanded one, but the gearhead held tight.

I tried to get up, but some force was keeping me down. "Ratchet, no! Uncle Artie, I won't leave you!" I crawled the other way along the catwalk, and I managed to stand up. The members of the Verge were dragging Ratchet along the path.

"Carlton! Go home! Find the Tick Tock Man. He's the only one who can help." He struggled to get away, but the Verge gearheads were winning, taking him over the handrail to the unknown area below. He grabbed the rail and pulled himself up. "The Tick Tock Man. He's your only chance." With a flick, he tossed his watch at me, and it landed on the catwalk.

"But where—?" They dragged him below before I could finish.

The last thing I wanted was to go down with him, so I picked up his watch and started running. I didn't look back as I went around the mainspring room and past the gong rods we had hidden behind a few minutes earlier. I nearly ran into someone shaped like a clock hand who refused to step aside.

The smell was gone, so I figured I had shaken the Verge,

or they didn't care about me. Either way, I kept going.

I finally turned to look when I arrived at the four-sided clock in the park. The catwalk was clear in both directions.

Now what?

The question buzzed through my head as I tried to catch my breath. Then I opened my hand and saw Ratchet's watch. I took mine from my pocket and examined it. Both knobs were pushed in. That's how we got here. So the only logical way to get back was ...

I pulled both knobs up at the same time. I was instantly back in my house in the center of the isochronal circle. The timepieces stopped swirling and fell to the ground with a *thud.* My legs started to give out, so I plopped on the nearby couch. A thousand thoughts battled it out in my brain, but I narrowed it down to three big problems.

Battling factions in Furtwangen.

Ratchet taken by the Verge.

Need to find the Tick Tock Man.

I had no idea how to solve any of these. I punched the couch cushion as hard as I could. Then I punched it again. And again. And again.

Thanks a lot, Uncle Artie.

Or Ratchet.

Or whoever the heck you are.

CHAPTER NINE

I felt a little better being home and knowing I was safe from the Verge. At least, that's what I thought. I went to the kitchen and grabbed a bottle of water from the refrigerator. Normally, I wasn't much of a water drinker, but that final dash left me parched, and I quickly gulped it down. All the excitement left me hungry too, so I grabbed a quick bite to eat. I always found I could think better on a full stomach.

As I gobbled down some cake, I thought about the three big problems. The battling factions seemed like an issue that had been around for many years and I likely couldn't fix that one. Ratchet was taken by the Verge, but he could probably hold his own until I knew more. That left only one. The one Ratchet screamed to me. *Find the Tick Tock Man*. The name was perfect for the situation I was currently in. Who wouldn't trust a guy with a cool name like the Tick Tock Man? But where would I find him?

I had to be careful whom I trusted, according to Ratchet. Then it came to me.

Fuzee.

I had met her only the one time, but she was helpful. It seemed like a long shot that I could even find her in that crazy clock world—I mean Furtwangen—but I had to try. The isochronal circle was certainly an option for getting back, but I wasn't sure if I trusted where it took me or even if I could make it spin.

Then I remembered the old Baptist church and going "inside" its clock tower. That's where I saw her last. It was worth a shot.

I left the timepieces in a circle in case I needed them later on. If Mom came home and found them, I'd just make something up. By that time, I would probably have worse problems anyway.

I jumped on my bike and headed to the old Baptist church with renewed energy. I put the bike out of sight behind a large bush and stood beneath the clock tower. As before, I placed my left hand on the white shingles and used my right to pull out the knob. The watch spun quickly. There was an odd vibration, and I could feel the presence of Fuzee and the Sequence and Furtwangen. The feeling was different than at the old Baptist church. This was more of a hallway than a door. I pushed the knob at two and felt myself being pulled in.

Then I *was* in.

I got my bearings and saw the large gears in front of me and to my left. The last time I was here I headed past them and ran into Fuzee. It seemed like the way to go. I ducked past the gear rods and set off along the catwalk, keeping my eyes, ears, and nose open for signs of the Verge. Running into them would be bad news.

Just before I came to the next clock on the path, a small voice called out, "CJ?"

I turned and saw Fuzee coming up the path, her round face practically glowing as she flashed a wide smile.

"Fuzee! I'm so glad I found you. I need your help."

Her smile turned to a serious look as she stood beside me. "You shouldn't be here. It's quite dangerous."

"I know. The Verge took my friend, the one we call Ratchet Dog. Do you know him?"

She eyed the path in both directions. "Yes. I've heard of Ratchet Dog. Some call him RD. I'm sorry they took him, but you must leave right this minute."

Ratchet Dog's initials were RD. That explained Uncle Artie. Very clever. "I have to find him. He needs my help. He told me to look for the Tick Tock Man. Do you know who that is?"

Once again she looked around nervously, then turned her head to listen for something. "We cannot stay here. Follow me."

She took my hand and led me down a side path, which cut dangerously close to the clock's main wheel. A small stairway took us under the second wheel. Fuzee was small and had no trouble ducking under and around the clock parts, but I banged my head on a spring barrel and stopped to rub it.

"Come on." She pulled me by the arm. Fuzee was stronger than she looked. We came to a ladder, and she let me go first. I couldn't see where it landed, but I trusted her and started climbing into the cloudy, murky world far below the catwalk. Finally, my right foot hit solid ground, and I waited for Fuzee, who jumped down beside me. This time I grabbed her by the arm as I caught my breath.

"Where are we going?" I asked between gulps of air. "Please tell me it's Furtwangen."

"Yes. It's just down the path." She took my hand once again and started off. "It's not much farther."

The scenery, for lack of a better term, was similar to what

I saw just before Ratchet was taken. It was getting lighter and lighter the closer we got. A large, swinging pendulum appeared in the path, and we easily timed our way around it. The fog and mist began to lift, and a few steps later, we were standing in bright sunshine. Ahead of us was what looked like a small village, complete with colorful houses and shops. It reminded me of the cuckoo clock Ratchet gave us. A German village.

Furtwangen.

We finally stopped when we got to a small park on the edge of the village. We rested on a short wall that surrounded a colorful garden in the center of the park. A large clock on top of an ornate pole was directly in front of us.

The time was stopped at two, just like on all the other clocks.

"Are we safe?" I asked. "Can the Verge find us?"

Fuzee stood and dusted off her cone-shaped dress. "They rarely venture into town. Their power is strongest in the Sequence."

"This is Furtwangen, right?"

"Yes."

I remembered Ratchet telling me about the two factions. It seemed like a good idea to drop the names. "Is this the Kinzig or Murg side?"

She stepped away from me like I was suddenly poisonous. "Which side are you on?"

Her oversized eyes burned a hole in me. I knew it was important to say the right thing, right now. I had a fifty-fifty shot at getting it right. "Kinzig, of course."

Fuzee's smile returned, and I exhaled heavily. "The Murgs are the cause of all the problems," she said. "You would be wise to avoid them."

Being in the middle of a conflict between the Furtwangen folks was not my idea of a good time. We did appear to be safe, however, and I felt comfortable and confident getting more information from Fuzee. "Have you heard of the Tick Tock Man?"

Her eyes did a really weird thing. They started spinning like gears as she appeared to be thinking about my question. The right one stopped first, then the left, sort of like a slot machine. I guessed that meant she had an answer. "I have not heard of this man. Whom does he represent?"

The whole "represent" thing was kind of unclear to me. "I don't know. My friend Ratchet told me to find him. He's the only one who can help."

This produced more spinning eyeballs but only for a few seconds. Just when I thought she was mostly human, she went all machine on me. "There is someone nearby who may know." She took my hand and led me down the brick path toward the village. I couldn't tell if she held on to me because she liked me or because she didn't want me to get away. I was fine with either reason. Her hand was warm and moist, just like mine.

The village houses were tiny, and they looked like they came right off the front of a cuckoo clock. They were A-shaped except for a flat top, and each had a balcony, large front windows, and oversized wooden doors. The grass next to the sidewalk was perfectly cut, and every flower box was bursting with multicolored blooms. There was no sign of trash anywhere. It was a miniature paradise.

We turned a corner and headed down another road, this one lined with small shops and stores. Most of them were light-colored, with dark crisscrossing boards on the front. I looked down the lane and put the brakes on, pulling Fuzee hard to make her stop too.

Pendulums. Hundreds and hundreds of them in a line as far as I could see. Nothing appeared to be holding them up, just tall, brass pendulums with massive bobs—the round part at the bottom—swinging at different speeds.

"Murg is just over there," Fuzee said with a finger extended. "We're free to move around, but danger lurks on the other side."

We kept walking down the path, past shop after shop. A lone shopkeeper swept the stone path in front of his shop without looking at us. We hit the end of the path and saw three small trails heading toward the border.

"So, where is this person who can help us find the Tick Tock Man?"

"There," she said, pointing to the many large pendulums. "We must travel to the Murg side."

"But I thought you said it was dangerous." I barely had enough spit to swallow, but I managed.

"It is the only way to find the one you are looking for. Besides, I can protect you."

Fuzee was a full head shorter than me—maybe four-and-a-half feet tall—and she was going to protect *me*? She looked at me with those large, reassuring eyes and took my hand. There was something about her, something that made me trust her. Ratchet told me to be careful, but I went with my gut feeling. I felt a connection. "Okay," I said. "Let's go."

She took us down the path on the right. It looked like cobblestone, but it sure felt like we were following the Yellow Brick Road.

CHAPTER TEN

I thought we were heading toward the crazy pendulum wall that divided Furtwangen, but we took a quick right turn off the path and headed into the darkness at the edge of town. Fuzee kept her strong grip on my left hand. It seemed like she was intent on protecting me. I mean, what else could it be? How could she like me when she barely knew me?

"Why are we going this way?" I asked. "Murg is over there." I motioned to the many swinging pendulums.

"It's nearly impossible to maneuver around the pendulums. Many have tried and failed. The edges are razor sharp. I know another way through the Sequence that is much less dangerous."

We came to the edge of the village, and everything turned

foggy and misty again. She held my hand tightly until we came to another path inside the Sequence. We glided along the handrail for a few minutes before reaching the familiar catwalk. The inner workings of a large clock stood before us, but I couldn't tell which one. My heart started to race knowing we were heading to the Murg side.

Fuzee pressed on ahead of me, seemingly unfazed by everything. I could hear strange noises and odd grunts coming from every direction. I thought I heard a grinding noise.

"What if we run into the Verge?" I asked. "They took Ratchet without too much trouble."

We stopped to rest. She stood in front on the walk while I sat up on the rail. More citizens passed by without incident.

"I can protect you." Her head turned in quick jerks, like she was scanning the place. "Besides, they don't come to this area very often."

"Why not?"

"There are some things I just can't explain, CJ of the Hoffhalder. You'll have to trust me."

I did trust her, even though I knew virtually nothing about her. I found it interesting that she referred to me as CJ of the Hoffhalder instead of just CJ. Maybe she had a title too.

"So what do you do in Furtwangen?" I asked as we started back along the catwalk.

"What do you mean?"

"I mean do you have a job or a title or a family? Anything?"

"I am Fuzee."

I wanted to keep the conversation going but not in circles. I needed something, anything from her. I thought of the question she asked me. "Who do you represent?"

She stopped, and I bumped into her small but solid frame. Her eyes spun, but only for a second or two. "I represented the Urgos."

I had heard the name before when I was doing some clock research. It was famous name in German clockmaking. Wait a minute, did she say *represented?*

"What happened to the Urgos?"

"It was replaced many years ago. I'd rather not talk about it."

We saw no one else along the path as we continued at our brisk pace. Fuzee seemed determined to help me, so I decided to try to help her too.

"Can you leave this place?"

"Why would I want to leave?"

"There's another world out there. My world. And when we're done here you should come back with me."

Her curly hair shook furiously. "I … I cannot."

"But why? I know a place on the other side of Furtwangen. We can get out—"

"I used to live out there. It was many years ago."

Now we were getting somewhere. I was thrilled to know she used to be just like me. I pressed on. "Where did you live?"

She stopped on the catwalk, but this time I slammed into her and bounced onto the ground. She never budged. "I don't want to talk about it, Carlton James."

"How did you know my real name? I never mentioned it. Not once."

Her eyes seemed bigger than ever as she stood over me. "I know many things."

I had so many more questions to ask, but my brain was working faster than my mouth. I stood and steadied myself against the handrail. Little Miss Spitfire never blinked as she stared me down. My mom used that same look, and it meant "zip it." Must be a girl thing.

Then I heard the distinctive sound and smelled the sick, sour scent of the Verge. A gearhead appeared from behind a wheel just ahead of us. Another came up the path behind us. We were surrounded.

"Stay close to me," Fuzee said. "And do exactly what I say."

We continued along the path toward Gearhead Number One. She reached behind, and I took her hand. Either she was going to get us out of this, or, well, I going to end up with Ratchet. Or worse.

The gearhead stood his ground in front of us and the other stopped and held the rails. Fuzee released my hand. "Grab the rail and hold on!"

I did.

With a blur, she began to spin. The force lifted her off the ground, and she headed straight toward the Verge member in front of us. They collided with a spray of sparks, and the gearhead flew off and vanished over the rail. Wow! Fuzee had a few tricks up her slender sleeves.

She stopped spinning and stood between me and the other, even larger opponent. "Get behind the cogwheel and duck down. Go!"

I took off up the path and saw the large, slowly turning wheel to my left. I jumped the rail and found a small niche where I could still see the action. The gearhead moved in a confident manner toward Fuzee with his thumbs looped in the straps of his black overalls. She began to spin like before, but she only bounced off the much larger opponent. The gearhead showed no emotion as the sparks flew harmlessly off him.

This was not good. Not good at all.

Fuzee stopped spinning and retreated to a spot near me, just behind a large wheel. "Stay here," she whispered to me.

The gearhead approached. He stood directly in front of another large gear and finally showed some emotion. He smiled.

He ventured too close to the gear, and Fuzee sprang into action. She spun and connected with the cogwheel in front of us. In turn, that cause another wheel to spin, and the poor gearhead never had a chance. The gear pulled him down and began to grind away at his center. As more sparks flew, Fuzee switched direction and sent our nemesis from the Verge flying over the rail and into whatever lay beyond it. Then it got eerily silent.

"Where did you learn to do that?" I asked, still too scared to come out from hiding.

She smoothed the surface of her dress as if she had done nothing more than come in from a stiff wind. "I said I could protect you. That is all you need to know."

Okay, so the mystery-that-is-Fuzee would continue. I figured she'd earned that much after such an awesome display of self-defense.

We came to small path to the left, and she listened carefully, her eyes spinning like crazy. With a nod of her head, she gestured me to follow, and I was one step behind her.

"This will take us where we want to go," she said. "His name is Strike. He is a keymaster."

A keymaster sounded important, so I left it at that. And the name "Strike" didn't surprise me, either. That was the sound a clock makes when it counts the hour. I didn't have to look it up. I just knew it.

We emerged from the shadowy fringe of the Sequence and stepped through a tall hedgerow into the sunlight. Before us was another pristine-looking village.

Murg.

It didn't seem all that different from Kinzig. The houses and sidewalks and flower boxes were all perfect, the streets were wide, and the signs were wooden. Another German village lost in time. Everyone I had met told me Murg was the "other" side, so I kept that in mind as we moved about. I also remembered that these two villages were "warring factions." Funny thing was, no one seemed to be warring except for the occasional outburst from the Verge. If it was behind the scenes, they did a heck of a job of hiding it. Then again, nothing surprised me in Furtwangen.

I only got a small chance to check out Murg. We walked along the cobblestone street in front of several shops as Murgs went about their day. It looked remarkably like Kinzig. Fuzee slowed down in front of each door as if she was scanning them. She probably was. The fourth shop got her attention, so we stopped.

"This is the place," she said. "Help is just inside."

She took my hand and led me through the wooden door. It was short and squeaked loudly as it swung open. The room we entered was pitch black.

"Please lock the door behind you," said a voice from somewhere in the room. Fuzee slid the deadbolt and pulled on the door handle to be sure. It was locked tight.

The room lit up, slowly at first, then to a normal level. The walls were covered with keys. There were large keys, small keys, clock keys, door keys, and keys that opened who-knows-what. In keeping with the pattern I found in Furtwangen, the slender gentleman behind the counter in front of us resembled a key, sort of.

"Fluzee!" He held his stubby arms out and leaned over the counter. "So good to see you."

He had a thick German accent, but I understood everything. I wanted to laugh at his calling her "Fluzee," but I caught myself. Fuzee made no attempt to shake his hand or hug him or anything. Maybe they didn't do that sort of thing around here.

"Strike, this is CJ. A friend of mine," Fuzee said. "He represents the Hoffhalder."

Strike stood and gave me a good once-over. His head was shaped like an old-fashioned key—two giant circles mashed together—and he had to catch himself from falling onto the counter. I held out my hand, and he shook it. He looked mostly human except for his weird key-shaped head.

"Zee Hoffhalder," he said. "Yes, I have heard of you." He immediately turned to Fuzee. "So, Fluzee, tell me why you are here."

"CJ seeks the one known as the Tick Tock Man. Have you heard of him?"

Strike turned his gaze to me. "Why do you seek this man?"

"My friend Ratchet told me to find him. Ratchet was captured by the Verge earlier today. He said the Tick Tock Man is the only one who can help."

He leaned toward me and made a low grunting noise.

"Wait a minute," I said. "Are you, by chance, the Tick Tock Man, Strike?" It was worth a shot asking.

He let out a weird laugh and clanged a bit as he shook. Many of the keys covering the walls shook with him. "No. I have been called many things but never that. I am a keymaster; nothing more. Tell me what exactly Ratchet asked of you."

"I told you. He said to find the Tick Tock Man."

Strike twisted his key handle-shaped head and focused

one, huge eye on me. His peepers were even larger than Fuzee's.

"Anything before that?"

I thought back to the last time I saw Ratchet. "Hey, you're right. He said, 'Go home and find the Tick Tock Man.'"

Fuzee and Strike laughed together, and the whole place began was filled with clanging and banging and the occasional chime. Strike sat back on his chair behind the desk and the room went silent. "We cannot help you," he said. "You, on the other hand, can help us a great deal. Our clocks will stay silent as long as our problem remains."

"So what exactly is the problem? No one ever told me."

Strike looked over at Fuzee, who put her head down, like she was in shame. "You have not told him?"

Fuzee meekly shook her head.

"Told me what? Somebody please fill me in."

Before Strike could answer, Fuzee stepped between us. "It is the mainspring, the most important piece of equipment in all of Furtwangen. It disappeared at precisely two of the clock yesterday. The Murgs are blaming the Kinzigs, and the Kinzigs are blaming the Murgs."

Well, that explained why all the clocks stopped. Now all I had to—

The place began to shake like nothing I had ever felt

before. The walls chimed and gonged and dinged, and Strike fell off his chair and disappeared behind the counter.

"Leave now!" Strike yelled from his fallen spot.

Fuzee grabbed my arm and pulled me toward the front door. We quickly left and went behind the shop. A small path led to the edge of Murg, and Fuzee sped down it with me in tow.

"What was that sound?" I asked between gulping breaths.

"The battle has begun. You must leave, and I must get back to Kinzig. This path will take us to a place you know. We must hurry."

She sped up, and so did I. We pushed through the barrier and arrived at the familiar catwalk that ran through the Sequence. After a quick left turn—well into Murg country, I mentally noted—we came to a clock movement and clock face I didn't recognize, at least not from the inside.

Another distant explosion rocked the catwalk, and I held on to the handrails as the whole thing swayed.

"Go! I will try to find Ratchet Dog and help him. You must help us. Find—"

Something zoomed down the path and knocked Fuzee off the catwalk. She started to fall, then began to spin like mad and rose back up. "Find the Tick Tock Man." Then with a blur, she zoomed down the path toward Kinzig.

I ducked behind the chimes and found a comfortable spot. So much stuff was flashing through my mind, making it difficult to concentrate. I placed my left hand on the wall and hoped my "two o'clock" method would once again get me back to my world. Seconds later, I was standing behind the bank, touching the clock tower. No one saw me.

I sprinted to the old Baptist church a few blocks away and found my bike. As I pedaled, I wondered which world was real. My world was calm and serene and peaceful. Furtwangen was suddenly in utter chaos. How could this be happening?

It didn't matter because I would do whatever it took to help Fuzee and the others. I had to save them.

I would save them. I was sure of it.

CHAPTER ELEVEN

I ditched the bike on the lawn and sprinted to the front door. It was still open, so I flew through it and headed straight to the living room. The timepieces were still in a circle on the floor where we left them, so I was relieved to know that no one had come home while I was gone. And how long was I gone? I checked the digital clock and saw that only two minutes had passed since I left. I didn't understand how that could have happened, but it didn't matter.

The idea of going back to Furtwangen using the isochronal circle was just too risky, so I put all the clocks back where I found them, as if it had never happened. I kept rolling through the day's earlier events as I hung up or replaced each timepiece. Somewhere in the circle formed by all the great town clocks was someone known as the Tick Tock Man, and I had to find him. Unfortunately, I had no idea where to start.

When in doubt, check the Internet. That was one of my mottos, and it had come through for me lots of times. I took out my laptop and searched for clockmakers and clock repair shops in the immediate area.

Nothing.

There were a few up to twenty miles away, but those hardly counted. I was sure the Tick Tock Man was close. But how to find him? Then I remembered one of my mom's old standbys: the phone book. I found an old copy of the Yellow Pages and began to thumb through it.

Cleaning services. Climbing Schools. Clinics. Finally I came to Clocks. At least there were a few entries to consider. All of them were in neighboring towns.

Except one.

The Clock Shop.

It was the smallest entry under clocks, and it only had an address and telephone number. No advertisement on the page, unlike most of the others. Nothing fancy. Was this the home of the real Tick Tock Man? I had to find out.

I wrote the address on a piece of paper and tucked it into my jeans pocket. There was no indication if The Clock

Shop was even open on the day after Thanksgiving, but I was willing to find out.

My bike was still on the front lawn, and I hit the pavement within a few seconds. I was sure the shop was going to be located smack in the middle of the clock face, but the road took me to the general direction of the nine. This was the old part of town, as my mom called it, and the buildings were squished together and right on the sidewalk. I took out the paper and checked the address: 33 Barron Road. The odd-numbered buildings were on the left, so I checked the addresses closely as I slowly rode by. I saw 49 and 45. Number 41 was a small coffee shop and 35 an antique store.

Then 29. I braked and skidded to a stop. What happened to 33? I leaned my bike against a light pole and checked it out by foot. Next to the alley was the antique store with a gold 35 in the window. Then an old door, then a dry cleaner at 29.

The old door. I checked the window and in letters that were barely readable, I saw:

THE CLOCK SHOP. CLOCKS CLEANED AND SERVICED

Some letters were fading so it looked like:

CLOCKS LEANED AND SERVED

The doorknob was large and cold, and it squeaked like it hadn't been oiled in years. The old door groaned at the hinges as I opened it and stepped inside. There was no shop, only a steep staircase with barely any light to guide me.

This can't be good for business, I thought as I started up the noisy stairs. Everything about this place seemed like it was out of the 1950s. Or older. My steps echoed as I continued up. I tested the rail, and it was a bit loose, not surprisingly. The door at the top of the stairs was dark with frosted glass on top and a mail slot below. I had seen these kinds of entrances in old movies. I turned the knob and slowly opened the door, half expecting some cigarette-smoking private detective to be at his desk on the other side.

It was definitely a clock shop! The room was filled with ticking and clicking and the occasional chime. There was a long counter in front of me, and the entire right side was lined with every conceivable type of clock, each with a small, white tag hanging from it. I figured that must be where the fixed ones go. Behind the counter and along the wall was a line of grandfather clocks, their pendulums gently swinging.

It took a few more seconds, but it finally struck me. The times on these analog clocks were correct. All the others in town were stuck at two, but these ticked right along.

That was a good sign.

I thought by now someone would come out to help me, but it was just me and the clocks. There was no bell or buzzer to ring or number to take, so I waited a few more seconds.

After spending most of the morning in Furtwangen, my clock patience was starting to grow thin. I cleared my throat to get someone's attention. Then I knocked on the counter. No one showed up.

"Hello?" I called, but not too loudly. "Hello?" Louder that time.

Finally, I heard a noise from the back room as a door closed somewhere. Then a woman came out from behind a dark curtain. She was in her twenties, maybe, with dark hair pulled back. She wore a blue apron, looking like she was ready to cook something.

"I'm sorry to keep you waiting. A shipment just arrived, and I was called away." She looked me over from top to bottom, then put both palms down on the counter. "So, how may I help you?"

Her eyes messed me up. There was something about them, something familiar. They were dark and large. Not Fuzee-sized, but pretty darn big. I forced myself to stop staring.

"I'm CJ." It was all I could come up with before my mouth refused to cooperate.

"Hi, CJ. I'm Adele. How may I help you?"

I focused on the large clock directly behind her. It seemed to help because the words finally came to me. I knew it was rude not to look her in the eyes, but I couldn't. "This might seem like a weird question, but I'm looking for someone who goes by the name of the Tick Tock Man."

"Is this some sort of joke?"

"Well, no, it's just that—"

"Do you go into a tire store and ask for the rubber man? Or the book store and see if the paper man is there?"

"Well, I—"

"It's a clock shop. Clocks go 'tick tock' so there must be a tick tock man here, right?" She leaned over the counter and glared at me with those menacing eyes. I tried to look away, but she was locked on me like a laser.

There was something about her eyes that made me keep looking. They were more than just dark brown circles. They had tiny bobs attached to the top. They were ... pendulums. That meant she was one of them. Or one of us. I didn't matter because I knew she could help me.

"I certainly hope so, Adele. You see, after Ratchet was taken by two members of the Verge, I got Fuzee to take me from Kinzig to Murg to see Strike, the keymaster. Unfortunately, he couldn't help. Are you following?"

"Well, I—"

"Did I mention that I represent the Hoffhalder? That's probably important, since it's also missing. Anyway, I used an isochronal circle to gain access to the Sequence. Boy, is that a fun place to be. But my point is this: the mainspring is missing, and all the clocks in town except for these are stuck at two o'clock. The only person who can help me goes by the name of the Tick Tock Man." This time I did the leaning. "You know who he is, Adele." One final lean. "I have to find him."

The stare-down lasted only a few seconds. She backed away and bumped into a grandfather clock. She tried to speak, but she could only tilt her head sideways. She put one finger in the air. "Wait here."

Adele went back through the same door she entered. The room grew silent save for the constant ticking, only now the ticks were synchronized. It was definitely not that way when I came into the shop. The rhythmic clock sounds were interrupted a few minutes later by some back-room noise. There were a few clangs, several bumps, and what clearly sounded like hammering on the wall. Adele emerged from the doorway, looking slightly flustered. She nearly tripped on something before straightening herself out.

"This way." She moved her hand toward the back of the shop. I didn't see an obvious way around the counter, so I plopped myself on it and swung my feet to the other side. Adele was already heading to the back of the store, so I picked up the pace and met her just before we took a hard right next a workbench filled with hands and pendulums and other small clock parts. At the end of the small hallway was another door, only this one opened in the middle. It was an elevator.

"I have to stay up here and mind the counter," Adele said with little emotion. "Take this elevator to the ground floor."

The elevator door opened quietly, and I walked in. When I turned around, Adele was gone and the door closed. I pressed the G button.

It was without a doubt the slowest elevator in the world. It shook and bucked as it made its way a whole ten feet, or so. The lights dimmed a bit before we came to a not-so-smooth stop. I steadied myself against the back wall. *Please don't let me die in here.*

The door opened three inches then stopped. Was I supposed to pry it the rest of the way? I tried and eventually spread the doors enough to get through. On the way down, I had time to wonder what might be waiting for me on this floor. I wondered if I was finally going to meet the famous Tick Tock Man and get to the bottom of this situation. Now was my chance.

The ground floor wasn't much different from the upper floor. There were boxes and clocks and parts everywhere in the narrow hallway. I walked past a double door on my right with a red EXIT sign above it. It probably led to the street and was how all this stuff got in here. There was a door at the end of the hallway, which seemed like my only possible destination. Like everything upstairs, this door was from another place in time. To make things even creepier, there was nothing written on the frosted glass. I took a deep breath and turned the oversized knob. The springs groaned and clicked but finally gave way. I swung the door open, and I saw only an empty room. All that work getting here, and this is what I get? Such a letdown.

"Hello? Anybody here?" I moved to the center of the room for a better look. The view was the same from every angle. Nothing.

I started to turn when something caught my eye. A large clock slowly appeared on the wall in front of me. Its loud ticking filled the room. Then clocks started popping up all over, and in seconds, the entire room was lined with clocks of all shapes and sizes. They all began to tick in sequence. I wanted to run, but my legs wouldn't move. The clocks ticked louder and louder until the sound completely filled my head. Just when I thought I couldn't take anymore, they stopped completely.

The door on the left side of the room opened, and a small man in a wheelchair slowly rolled into the room.

I had found the Tick Tock Man.

CHAPTER TWELVE

He guided his wheelchair right toward me. The old man wore neither a smile nor a frown. He had on brown pants, a brown shirt, and brown shoes, like one of those UPS guys. What little hair he had was combed straight back to make his head look like half a Q-tip. I couldn't help but notice his oversized glasses made his eyes look huge. Having mega-peepers seemed to be a popular trait among these clock people. I guess that was necessary for looking at all those tiny parts.

His wheelchair stopped mere inches from my toes. He sighed and looked up at me with soft, blue eyes. "It's about time you got here."

That was so not what I had expected. I took a step back

to gather my thoughts. This would be a bad time to say something stupid. "What do you mean?" I managed to say.

His gaze never left me. "I mean I've been expecting you, Carlton. We have issues, you know. Lots and lots of issues."

It was odd that he called me Carlton. He must have gotten it from Ratchet. Anyway, I figured it was best to go with what I knew and see if it made stuff any clearer. It certainly couldn't get any worse. "The clocks in the town are all stuck at two o'clock, and the people of Furtwangen are having some sort of conflict. Only the Tick Tock Man can fix everything. And you, sir, are the Tick Tock Man."

He waved his right hand in the air in front of me. "I don't know who comes up with these names. I, for one, have always hated that particular title. It's degrading to clocks everywhere. Wouldn't you agree?"

"Sure. I'll go with that. Mister, um … so what do I call you?"

"Albert Nagel." He held out his right hand and I gave it a firm shake. His grip could have crushed my hand if he wanted it to. "Never understood the whole Tick Tock Man label. Clocks are complicated objects with thousands of parts. Besides, very few of them actually tick and tock." He placed his handle gently on his lap. "Sorry, I tend to ramble a bit."

There was a small stool a few steps away, and I motioned

to it. "Okay if I have a seat, Mr. Nagel?"

"Sure. But don't be so formal. I'm Albert, and you're Carlton." He cleared his throat. "Moving on." He wheeled himself over to a workbench where clock parts were spread out everywhere. He clicked on a desk lamp.

I sat down and quickly reassessed my plans. He was not what I expected, but I was happy with what I was seeing. I needed answers but so many questions swirled around in my brain. I decided to start with the basics. "So what's going on, Albert?"

"What do you mean?"

"Why are all the clocks in town except the ones in your shop stopped at two o'clock?"

He was peering at the back of a clock using a magnifying light. He rotated the piece several times before placing it back down. "Are you sure it's all of them?"

"All the ones I've seen today, and I've seen a bunch."

"From what you told my assistant, you've had quite a day so far. True?"

"I've been to Furtwangen. I know all about the battling factions called Murg and Kinzig. I was asked to find you, and I did. Why did all the clocks stop?"

He hummed like he was busy at work, but I could tell he was ignoring me. "Lots of clocks," he said. "So many clocks.

Who's to know which are running and which aren't?" He hummed some more. "So many clocks."

I couldn't take his stalling any more. I moved into his workspace and slammed my palm down under his magnifying light and yelled, "Why did all the clocks stop?"

He backed away from the workbench. "You are an extremely rude young man. You should leave." He completed the turn and faced the far wall with his head hung low. Did I go too far again? I couldn't leave now. I had to do or say something.

"Albert." There was a small stool near the workbench, so I sat on it to get a good look at him. "I'm sorry, okay? It's just that it's been a long day and so much has happened. I think once you hear what I've been through, you'll want to help." He didn't look up, but he didn't order me out again either. "It all started with the Hoffhalder."

I told him everything that had happened that day. His head came up when I mentioned Ratchet. He seemed to be interested in Fuzee and the Verge, and he laughed when I told him how she sent two of them over the rail. By the time I got to the conversation with Strike, he had rolled back to his favorite workspace and was looking right at me.

"So that's why I ended up here in your shop. Everyone seems to think you are the only one who can fix this mess.

But it all comes down to one question: why did the clocks stop?"

The room fell completely silent, except for the rhythmic ticking. Albert's breathing seemed to be timed to every third tick, like he was in sync with the room. *In* two-three, *out* two-three. That part didn't surprise me.

"Let me show you something." Albert moved a few feet toward the center of the room. "Step aside." I did as he said and took a spot near the workbench. He pointed at a small wall clock. It flew from the wall and followed the path of his finger before landing gently on the floor. An old-fashioned alarm clock was next, then a fancy glass clock, then a wristwatch. They went exactly where he commanded them— in a neat circle on the floor in front of us. A drawer next to me opened, and two more clocks joined in the fun. With the lift of his hand, they rose from the floor and began to spin.

"An isochronal circle," I said. "Ratchet showed me how to use one. It's how we got to Furtwangen this morning. I visited both villages."

"Very good. And tell me, did you notice anything unusual about Murg and Kinzig?"

The isochronal circle began to sparkle, so I put my hand up to shield against the light. "Unusual? Well, they were kind of old-fashioned looking."

With the swipe of his hand, the clocks spun even faster. The sparkles dissolved, and another image appeared. It was blurry at first; then one of the villages came into view. Yep, it was Kinzig, and it looked like we were seeing it through a snow globe. "Kinzig and Murg exist almost exactly as they did one hundred years ago." The image shifted to Murg, but it was hard to tell the difference between them. "They've had a century to fix their problems, but the problems still remain."

"What problems?"

Albert nodded to the isochronal circle, and it switched back to sparkle mode. "You see, an isochronal circle is not just a means of getting to Furtwangen; it is actual time travel. The power of the mainsprings makes it possible. It was outlawed many years ago because the village folks could not control their actions. They began to fight each other for control. Things got, shall we say, ugly."

"What happened?"

"My great-grandfather took the power away from the villagers and placed the great pendulum divide between them. Only a certain few are allowed to travel between the villages, and they do so at their own risk."

That made me think of Fuzee, and I couldn't help but hope she was all right. It seemed awfully dangerous for anyone to be traveling between villages. A quick recall of her spinning powers made me feel a little better.

"They were people once, weren't they?" I asked.

"Certainly. Each took on a particular characteristic. Time may have slowed, but evolution did not." The isochronal circle flashed images of several villagers, most of whom I'd never seen before. They were all an odd combination of human and clock parts. There were certainly some strange characters in the mix.

"Each side controls half the clocks in the towns," he continued, "but still they remain divided. Their century ended at two p.m. yesterday. They still have not resolved their issues, so I removed the mainspring. Perhaps now they will figure it out."

The clocks all struck the top of the hour and chimed at the same time. The noise was so loud I nearly jumped out of my chair. Albert remained calm as he waited for me to look at him. When the chiming stopped, he smacked the top of the workbench with his palm.

"That," he said with a slight smile, "is why the clocks stopped."

CHAPTER THIRTEEN

I was slightly relieved to know that I didn't cause all this by overwinding the Hoffhalder, or that I'd even overwound it at all. It was just a giant coincidence. Now that I had a few more answers, I needed to find a solution. My new friend the Tick Tock Man appeared to be coming up a little short in that department.

Albert resumed work at his station and seemed fully focused on ignoring me. I understood that the villagers had to solve their own problems, and it was up to me to pass on that information. Such fun.

The isochronal circle started spinning again, and I watched as the familiar image of Ratchet appeared in the middle of it. He was tied to a large gear, bound at both his feet and hands. As the gear turned, Ratchet turned with it. He smiled then swore loudly at the two members of the Verge who were guarding him. Albert wanted me to know Ratchet was still alive, and I was thankful for that. I had a feeling I would get a chance to help him very soon.

Without turning around, Albert summoned the circle to stop, and the clocks fell gently to the floor. The image of Ratchet faded away.

"Thanks, Albert." I walked toward the door.

He grunted something; then all the clocks flew up off the floor and went back to their original spots. The clock parts found their drawers and bins, and everything was returned to normal. I reached for the doorknob and twisted it, causing the entire door to shake from the squeak of the springs. As I looked back, the clocks in the room began to disappear, and soon it was as empty as the moment I entered it.

Except for Albert. He wheeled toward the door on the left with smooth strokes. The door opened, but instead of going through it, he gave me one last look. "The clocks have all stopped, and soon everyone in our town will notice. Your friends in Furtwangen can only fool them for so long."

"So what happens if the clocks don't get running again?"

"You don't want to know." Albert pushed his wheelchair toward the door, but I ran over and stopped him.

"Actually, I do." He tried his best to wheel away, but I held firm. "Please, Albert. I've come this far."

"Fine. Please release me." I took a step back, trusting that he would give me an answer. "The town clocks form the world's largest isochronal circle. You've seen the power of such a circle on a small scale, so just imagine the power of one the size of this town. We'll all be sent back a hundred years, give or take. If we survive it."

He wheeled through the door shaking his head the entire time. The room was now completely empty.

I didn't feel like going back up the creepy elevator or seeing creepy Adele in the shop, so I opened the small door that I hoped led outside. Sunlight began to peek in as it opened into the back alley. Finally, some fresh air. I took several deep breaths as the door closed behind me.

I ran out of the alley to the front of the building to find my bike. I was relieved to know it was right where I left it. The ride home would give me time to think, time to plan, time to figure this whole thing out. The images came too fast! Murg and Kinzig. Fuzee. Ratchet held prisoner. I could barely see the road in front of me. The Verge. Strike, the keymaster. The giant pendulums. It all seemed too much to fit in my head. My hands gripped the brakes, and I squeezed. It was time for a personal intervention.

"Stop, stop, stop!"

I yelled so loudly a woman walking nearby gave me a strange look. My legs locked to keep my bike and me from falling over near the curb. This was no time to be losing it, I thought. I needed to get my act together, and quickly.

What I needed was a plan.

For most of the day, just thinking that I needed a plan or idea or inspiration resulted in something positive happening. They just popped into my mind and off I went. Fat, dumb, and happy, as my dad always said.

I knew *what* I had to do. Knowing was the easy part. Just get the two warring factions to settle their differences—something they hadn't been able to do for many, many years—and all would be well. The clocks would start running, Fuzee would be forever grateful, and I'd be one of those "local heroes" I've read about in the paper.

Oh, I almost forgot. I also had to rescue Ratchet from whatever jail he was being held in. And I had to battle the Verge. And I had no idea how much time I had to do all this.

This was one of those mental lists with two columns of information. The *what to do* column was getting bigger and bigger. The *how to do* column mocked me like a blinking cursor on a blank computer screen. I added another item to the first column: I had to go back to Furtwangen right now.

The other column would have to wait.

I got on my bike and started back home, but a familiar voice interrupted my pedaling.

"CJ!" Brad's too-small bike cut in front of mine, and I had to skid to a stop.

"Hey, Brad."

"I've been looking for you all afternoon. I texted you three times and even called your house. You know how I hate talking on one of those things."

Yeah, Brad wasn't much of a talker. "I've been busy. So what's up?"

"We need one more player for hoops. We have a game ready go over in Ripley Park."

"I can't. I'm grounded."

"You don't look grounded to me."

"Well, I sneaked out of the house to take care of some business. But I'm heading back now." I pulled back and started around his bike. He backed up and grabbed my handlebars.

"Still worried about the stupid clocks, aren't you?"

His grip was tight, and I thought about ripping is hand away. Instead, I simply thought about making my handlebars hot. I focused on nothing else as I stared him down. He released his grip and shook his hand to cool it.

"I'd love to play, but I have to go." I slipped past him and broke into a fast pedal.

"You have to get over this Hasselhoff thing," I heard him yell. "I mean, seriously!"

As I rode home, I actually added something to my mental *how to do* list. I needed Fuzee's help, and I convinced myself she was my biggest ally. She and Strike asked me to find the Tick Tock Man and I had. I added visiting Strike to the list. The right side was puny but getting there.

I was back home in just a few minutes, thankful no one had come home early. I leaned my bike against the rail and went in through the unlocked front door. The isochronal circle was the best and safest way back, so all I had to do was—

Then I remembered I had put all the clocks away. I smacked my left palm hard with my right hand several times. It stung, but it was a reminder of how dumb I was to put them all away, even though it seemed like a good idea at the time. Albert the Tick Tock Man had no such issues. He just summoned the timepieces from around his shop, and they formed the circle. Wouldn't that be great?

One of the clocks was on the wall directly in front of me. I did what Albert had done earlier and pointed to it. Then, with a flick of my finger, I willed it to a spot on the floor.

Nothing.

Okay, no problem, I thought. *Time for a do-over.* Using the same focus and concentration that allowed me to heat up the handlebars, I once again pointed to the wall clock. I could feel its internal parts turning and ticking through my finger. I flicked my finger to the empty spot on the floor, and the clock floated gently to the spot.

It worked!

Most of the clocks I needed were upstairs in the spare bedroom. From the foot of the stairs I pointed to the room and the box landed on the floor with a soft *thunk.* One by one, Ratchet's clocks followed my command and found a place in the circle. The saw-blade clock proved to be the most difficult, but it arrived with only a small scratch on the stair rail. Now, where were all the other clocks? Two were in the next room, so I moved to the doorway and raised them a few feet off the ground. They too joined the circle.

I pointed up the stairs to my parents' room and willed the old wristwatches to join us, and they did. The isochronal circle was complete.

But I didn't make it spin. Not yet. One of those plans I'd been waiting for finally popped into my mind. I heard the unmistakable voice of Ratchet as he was being taken by two members of the Verge.

"Every clock has a face, and behind every face, something is ticking," he reminded me.

His image faded away, and the sweet face of Fuzee, with her curly brown hair and huge eyes appeared before me. She said she used to represent the Urgos, but it was replaced. I didn't make the connection at the time. I had to know what really happened.

I found my laptop and brought it back into the living room. I did a search for Urgos and found it was a common name among old clocks. That was no help. I added our town name to the search and got a little more but not enough to answer my questions. Finally, I put in Urgos with our town and "replaced," and boom! There it was: a link to an old historical document describing famous landmarks in our town. The old Urgos clock was badly damaged when it was struck by lightning. It was too expensive to fix, so the town replaced it with a fancy new digital movement some thirty years ago. I found the map I had drawn with all the great clocks. According to the article, the Urgos used to occupy the three on the giant town clock face. The Great Northern Bank's clock, less than a block away from the Urgos, now occupied that spot.

Then it hit me. *That's why Fuzee can't return.* The clock she represented was destroyed. That seemed so … wrong. I smacked the table with my palm, causing the laptop to jump a bit. If I had a way to fix it, I would. But I had other problems to fix, so I put the Urgos way down on my mental list.

The timepieces formed an impressive circle on the carpet of the living room. I took Ratchet's watch from my pocket and held it in my left hand. Two deep breaths later, I was standing in the isochronal circle. I mimicked Albert and moved my hand in a circular motion. Immediately, the timepieces began to swirl a foot off the ground. What do you know? I didn't even need the watch. Like a conductor, I brought both hands up, and the swirling mass began to rise. Next came the sparkles. I focused hard on getting back to the Sequence so I could finish the task at hand.

With a final flash, I was gone.

CHAPTER FOURTEEN

It almost felt like home. I arrived in an area of the Sequence just behind a large clock. The gears had stopped, and the usual ticking sound was gone. Albert was right about that part—without the mainspring, the clock people couldn't keep them going any longer. The silence was eerie.

My first stop was at the three o'clock position on the town clock face to see if Fuzee was around. I tried to run as fast as I could along the catwalk, but there were more inhabitants than the before. They mostly ignored me as I passed them, but the path was narrow, and it wasn't a good time for anyone to take a fall over the rail. My nose was on high alert for telltale signs of the Verge. So far, the smell stayed on the musty side. I was loving the mustiness.

Fuzee always seemed to know when I was near, and I hoped this time would be the same. I had found that to be true of many folks in Furtwangen. They seemed to have a sixth sense when it came to everyday events. Most knew my name before I introduced myself. Some knew about events I never mentioned. It all added to the craziness of Furtwangen.

Fuzee was the perfect example. I came back to the Sequence with the hope of finding her somewhere in that circular madness. At about four o'clock on the big face, I heard her voice. Was this telepathy or some other method of communication? I wasn't sure. But it was her voice all right.

I followed her calling as far as I could along the catwalk. Sure, there was the usual collection of unusual types—springs and gongs and shafts—passing me both coming and going. I guess the "conflict" was stirring up activity everywhere in the Sequence and forcing folks to be on the move. The ones who didn't move proved to be the biggest issue. The scent of the Verge filled my nostrils as I crept along the catwalk near the guts of a large clock. Maybe one of them passed recently and went down a side path.

No such luck. A gearhead appeared from behind a chime and blocked my path. He was smaller than the others I had seen and appeared to be alone. Young and solo. The perfect combination for me. I knew I'd have to face off with one or more of these guys eventually. That time was now.

Problem was, I didn't entirely know the extent of my powers. I knew I had a unique skill because I could feel it.

The young gearhead came at me full speed, and I simply treated him like one of the clocks in my living room. I placed my arm straight out to stop him, and he halted in a lurch. Then I raised my arm slightly, lifting the gearhead off the catwalk. I flicked my pointed finger to the left, but I did it too fast, and he dropped back to the catwalk. He smiled and continued his charge, so once again I placed my arm out. He was just a few inches from my fingertips, so I raised him up slowly, knowing this would be my last chance. His feet squirmed, and his gear-shaped head began to spin, but I didn't stop. I lifted him up, up, and up, then sideways until he was well over the rail. He resisted with an annoying grinding sound.

Using just my finger, I dropped him into whatever awaited below the catwalk. The air was clean and silent, and I continued onward, happy knowing I could at least hold my own. I saw fewer and fewer locals as I jogged along the trail. I wasn't sure if that was good or bad, considering the old "safety in numbers" saying I had heard.

It was the strangest thing: I could feel Fuzee before I could hear her. She was nearby. The voice was faint at first, then crystal clear.

"CJ! Over here."

I stopped and turned to see her behind a brass center post, her head sticking out just enough for me to glimpse her large eyes. I took a step toward her, and she pulled me in the rest of the way, practically yanking my shoulder out of its socket. I had forgotten how strong she was.

"It's not safe out here," she said with a passing glance up the catwalk. "The Verge, they're everywhere."

"I know."

I recalled for her my recent encounter with the young gearhead. I thought my exploits would impress her, but she barely looked my way.

"Stay with me. I can protect you."

Hey, I can protect myself, I thought. But deep down, I knew she was right. I was fairly new at this, and she was an experienced "warrior." By the looks of things here in the Sequence, we would likely get tested sooner rather than later.

We ventured farther back in the clockworks, which were no longer moving. From a small seat we could see through the clock face to the town below. It was the clock in Ripley Park.

"The one who represents this clock was taken by three members of the Verge a short time ago," Fuzee said. "We're safe for a little while."

She took my hand, and it made me relax immediately. There was something about the feel of her skin that brought me down a notch just when I most needed it. It wasn't mechanical. It was definitely a human touch, and I needed it right then. We stared at each other for five, maybe ten seconds. She started to smile, then broke her gaze. "The Tick Tock Man. Please tell me you found him."

"As a matter of fact, I did. His real name is Albert Nagel and he's very old, and he runs the clock shop in town."

"So he can help us, right?"

"Not exactly."

"What do you mean?"

"Well, here's the thing. Albert told me your two villages have had some sort of feud for a hundred years. Then something about isochronal circles being used improperly. I guess what I'm trying to say is, he won't help you. You have to solve this yourselves."

Her eyes spun like mad, much faster than I had ever seen them. Either this was her way of dealing with stressful situations, or she was going to kill me. I hoped for door number one.

"We are doomed, then."

"You can't think that. I mean, all you have to do is bury the hatchet."

She gave me a confused look, which made me wonder if I used the hatchet phrase correctly.

"I mean, you have to forget the past and reason with them."

"Impossible," she said. "The Murgs cannot be reasoned with."

"But what about Strike? He's on the Murg side, and you seem to get along just fine with him. In fact, I can't tell the difference between Murgs and Kinzigs. I mean, you're just a bunch of clock parts, right?"

Her right hand came up and stopped inches from my face. I knew she could cause some serious damage is she truly wanted to. Her eyes didn't spin; they just glowed in sync with her heartbeat. They went back to normal, and she put her hand down. "Strike is a friend of mine, but he is not like the other Murgs. You don't understand anything."

"Then why don't you explain it to me. Why do you guys hate each other so much?"

Something or someone zipped past us quickly, causing the chimes to play a few notes.

"We can't stay in the Sequence. We have to return to the village and find Strike. He can tell you everything."

Before I could respond, she took my hand and yanked me out from behind the clockworks. The catwalk was clear to our left, so we took off as fast as we could, our feet clanging on the steel surface as we ran. I felt like a football running back, with Fuzee blocking for me. First one, then another catwalk occupant ducked into a side path when they saw us coming. It made me appreciate having Fuzee on my side.

"This way," she said. We took a small path to our right toward what I thought was the village of Kinzig.

We broke through the mist and fog at the edge of town and came to a thick grove of trees. She led me on a full-speed, zigzagging maneuver through the grove and appeared at the edge of Kinzig. My heart rate was up considerably, but that always happened when Fuzee was nearby. Finally, we came to a small bench and stopped to rest. At least, I needed to rest. I wasn't sure if she ever did.

The village was much livelier than the last time I visited. The main street was bustling with town folks, most of them randomly running from one shop to another.

"What are they doing?" I asked, pointing in the general vicinity of the ruckus.

"Things have gotten much worse since you left. It is our livelihood to keep the town clocks running, and we are no longer able to do so." A chime-shaped person ran at full speed toward a shop and missed the door completely, making a loud gong sound as he bounced off the wall and fell to the ground.

"You've had a hundred years to fix this, according to Albert."

"There is nothing to fix. It is the world we live in. The Murgs have their side, and we have ours. There are some who think we don't need outsiders interfering with our ways."

I slipped in front of her, blocking her way, realizing too late that this may have been a dangerous move. Fortunately, she stopped quickly and held her ground.

"Interfering?" I said. "You *asked* me to find the Tick Tock Man. Strike asked me to find him too. Heck, Ratchet's final words as a free man were to find the Tick Tock Man. Now that I've found him, you don't like what he has to say. Look at the chaos in your village." I spread my hands out, but she refused to look. Instead, she grabbed my hand and pulled me in another direction.

"But I thought Murg was that way," I said, with a pathetic attempt at pointing over my shoulder.

"It is. But the trail we took last time is probably being watched. I know a shortcut." She took us away from the village and into what looked like an orchard. The trees were all the same size and lined in neat rows. Beyond these were the thick clump of trees and dense brush. There were no visible trails leading into the clump. We stopped as Fuzee checked the area.

"What is this place?" I asked. "There's no way in."

I wasn't exaggerating. The brush was so thick we could barely walk. The stalks had large thorns, and soon I was caught in it and my legs started to bleed. She pulled me out, and we withdrew to the safety of the orchard.

"It's here somewhere, I just know it," she said.

"What's here?"

"The ogive."

"What's an ogive?"

"An entryway shaped liked an arch. There are only a few still remaining." She scanned the area with her extra-large eyes, which spun like mad as her head turned from side to side. "There!" She pointed into the blackness just a few degrees to our left.

"I don't see anything." It was the thickest brush we had encountered. No way could I make it through without a chainsaw. Even that would have been pushing it.

"Follow me." Fuzee started to spin; then she began cutting though the overgrowth, blazing a nice trail as she went. The brush and scrub and thicket were no match for her whirling, top-shaped body. After about thirty feet, she stopped in front of two trees with massive trunks. There was no chance of going through them. Instead, she took my hand, and we went around. On the other side was a stone archway cut into side of the hill. It was about six feet tall and not even that wide. A small creek flowed out of it and disappeared around a curve a few yards away.

"The ogive," she said. "It is the only safe way to get to Murg."

I leaned into the opening and saw nothing but darkness. The damp smell nearly made me gag. Was this the only way to get there? I turned to ask Fuzee, but she was already ankle deep in water, heading straight in. Like dozens of times before, she snatched my hand and took me along.

Into the blackness.

CHAPTER FIFTEEN

Cold, wet, and dark. Three of my least favorite features wrapped up in one. The water from the creek quickly filled up my shoes and froze my ankles as we slogged forth through the ogive. I couldn't do much about the cold and the wet, but boy, I sure wished I had a flashlight or the glow from a cell phone or even one of these primitive stick torches. Anything.

That call was quickly answered as Fuzee's eyes illuminated, bathing the tunnel in a soft glow. This allowed us to see the block walls to the sides and the stream up ahead.

"How far is this place," I asked, wiggling my toes to keep them warm.

We hit a deep part of the creek, and I sank up to the

middle of my shins. The water seemed to be flowing quicker.

"Not much farther," she said. "Just after the split."

I didn't know what a split was, but I did hope it arrived soon. Fuzee mostly kept her eyes down as she navigated us throughout the stream. This made it difficult to see ahead, but at least we were making progress. She pulled me to the left, where the water was shallow, and it allowed us to pick up the pace. Soon, we were walking on damp rocks with a small stream beneath us. It felt so good to be out of the cold water, at least temporarily.

"There," she said. Her eyes were forward, shining light on the split up ahead. It looked like a giant, creepy Y with most of the water coming from the right side of the split. I secretly hoped we were heading left.

My thoughts were interrupted by the sound of splashing. I turned to look, but the ogive behind us only let in a small amount of natural light. I could hear them, whatever they were, jumping into the water.

"Muskrats," Fuzee said without a trace of concern. "They're fairly harmless."

Fairly harmless?

Fortunately, the splashing stopped as we came to the split. She held tight and led me into the left channel. The bed was dry, and we increased our speed to a brisk walk. I took a peek behind us, and it was completely dark except for a small sliver of light poking through onto the stream.

It made me wonder. In fact, I couldn't figure out if we were closer to Murg or Kinzig. "Where does the other fork lead?" I pulled on Fuzee's arm to get her attention.

She stopped and shined a bit of light back on the stream. "That one goes to an area called Enz. It's a place neither village claims."

"Why not?"

She turned and pulled me along, but I resisted. Her glowing eyes practically burned mine. "It is a bad place."

More evasiveness on her part. This was starting to tick me off. I stared back into those glowing eyes and managed to make her blink. Well, it looked like a blink. "Just answer the question. How come nobody claims Enz?"

She stood tall before me and folded her arms like a human girl. I guess I got her attention. "The Verge has occupied Enz for as long as anyone can remember. They take our people there sometimes. The best thing to do is stay far, far away from it." She grabbed my shoulder. "We really need to go. Now!"

My mind was on Ratchet as we slogged along. The vision I saw in the clock shop showed me he was still alive and being held by the Verge. I replayed it again and again, and I knew I had to find him. I did not fear going to Enz.

"We're here," she said, jolting me out of my vision. We turned a corner, and a small amount of light came through another arch-shaped ogive. "Murg."

The top of the opening was covered with a moss-like plant that hung down several feet. I went first and parted the slimy stuff to allow Fuzee to walk through to the outside. Once out, we were faced with dense brush and trees much like we found at the entrance. I knew Little Miss Chainsaw would take care of that problem.

"Stand back." In a blur, she hacked a path through the foliage and came to rest behind a large formation of boulders. She peeked around the biggest one, and I leaned over her shoulder to get a look. Oddly enough, there wasn't a bit of bark or grass or any debris on her. *She must be self-cleaning,* I thought.

There was a lot of commotion going on in Murg, just like we had seen in Kinzig. The villagers were running around, many bumping into whatever was in front of them. Odd-looking clock parts came out of nowhere and disappeared behind doors or through windows. It reminded me of one of those old Westerns where everyone would scatter when the bad guys came riding in for a showdown.

"We need to get closer," Fuzee said in a quiet voice. I

considered bringing up the showdown scenario but thought better of it. She led me behind what looked like a stable, although I couldn't imagine anyone around here riding a horse. We sneaked in the back door, and I was pleasantly surprised to see it was a blacksmith shop, complete with a large furnace and bellows. We walked up a creaky set of stairs to a loft. From the high vantage point, I could see dozens of large clock hands leaning against the back wall. Fuzee led us along the wooden walkway to a single window overlooking the main road. She opened it, and we got a great view of the action below from our lofty perch. I couldn't begin to know how she found out about this place.

The real cause of the commotion was making its way down the main street on our right. Four members of the Verge walked in a straight line toward the center of the village. This caused more door slamming and window closing and general mayhem.

"What are they doing here?" I asked. "I thought you said they hung out in the Sequence."

"They usually do. We'll see the occasional renegade gearhead ramble through, but I've never seen a pack like this. Not in either village."

"What do they want?" My question caused her eyes to spin.

"I'm not sure. They thrive on chaos, but since we are a peaceful people, they find very little of it." A large, tubular chime-shaped Murg ran full speed in the direction of the Verge members. The largest gearhead stepped in front of it, and the chime bounced off and fell to the ground with a loud *bong*. Immediately the other gearheads began to grind away at the chime. It didn't have a chance.

"We have to stop them," I said.

"No." She put out her arm to hold me back. "There are too many. Plus, that's what they want."

"Oh, I see. It's okay for them go after the Murgs, right. I bet if they were attacking your Kinzig friends, you'd be singing a different tune."

She pulled me close, practically nose to nose. Her eyes looked bigger than ever. "That's not true, and you know it."

"Do I? You're not being too convincing."

More havoc below interrupted our talk. The Verge members were in the process of destroying the storefront of a small shop. They sawed through the front posts, collapsing the entrance roof.

"I can protect you, but not from four of them. If we wait, they'll just go away."

"Wrong. The real war has begun. I can feel it."

"So what do you suggest we do?"

I had already begun hatching a plan. I looked around the shop and saw what I needed. "I need you to go down the stairs and slide open the front door. Then I need you to get them away from the building and into the middle of the road. Do you think you can do that?"

Her eyes began to spin. That was usually a good sign. "You bet I can. What are you going to do?"

"You'll see. Just get them in the open and take cover."

She edged around me and took off down the stairs. The front door was one of those large, sliding types, like on a barn. I watched as she removed the security plank across the center and pulled with all her might. It barely budged. She rearranged her feet and tried again, straining as she pushed. This time the door cooperated and slowly began to open, filling the first floor with sunlight.

Then I went into action. There was still a hint of red in the forge fire, so I pointed my right index finger at the bellows and began to pump the top arm up and down. I got into a rhythm, and soon the fire was blazing. I took a quick look outside. Fuzee was yelling something at the gearheads. They stopped destroying the shop and turned their attention to her. They took a slow walk, staying in a pack, just like I wanted them. She began to spin and went in crazy circles around the foursome before hovering just out of reach over their heads.

It was time for the clock hands to help out. With just the flick of my wrist, I sent the first four out through the big door and onto the street. I made them spin crazy fast and moved them in a circle around the gearheads. Fuzee took the hint and got out of there and came back into the shop. She watched from the safety of a small window near the door.

The next batch of clock hands took a detour through the forge fire. It didn't take long to make the pointed tips glow red. I sent them out one by one in the direction of the gearhead circle. The Verge gang managed to avoid the first hand and even the second, but I kept them coming. As the four spinning hands kept the gearheads in a pack, the next wave of red-tipped hands found their mark. The first hand struck the smallest gearhead, knocking him to the street with a loud *clang*. The next one was also on target, and sent the biggest gearhead to his knees.

Then came the grand finale. I summoned every clock hand in the blacksmith shop to join in the fun. They flew out the door and came at the gearheads from all directions. They knocked a few away, but there were too many projectiles for them to defend. Hand after hand struck their bodies repeatedly until they couldn't get up. I moved two spinners from the back to the front line and formed a wall of four. The gearheads took the hint and began to leave the village the same way they arrived. I sped up the four spinners and made the intruders run as fast as they could until they were out of sight.

To make sure, I hurried down the stairs and out the door. Satisfied that they were gone for good, I brought back the spinning blades and returned all of them to their original spots.

"You were superb!" Fuzee said. "I have never seen the Verge run away from anything." She took my hand, yanked me toward her, and squeezed me harder than I had ever been squeezed. I was actually ready for it, and it felt kind of nice. Plus, I had never been called "superb."

The villagers began to leave the houses and shops. Murgs of all shapes and sizes lined the main street, most looking in the direction where the Verge had run. Others looked at the two of us in the middle of the street.

"Fluzee!" Strike pushed through the crowd, his key handle head towering over all the others. "Fluzee, so good to see you again." He joined us but stayed a short distance away, like I was contaminated or something. "And you, CJ. You have learned a few tricks, yes?"

Before I could answer, Fuzee stepped between us. "Have you ever seen the Verge get taken down like that? CJ here is my new hero." That earned me another hard squeeze.

"I'm just figuring out what I can do," I said. I figured staying humble would be the best way to go.

"We have much to discuss," Strike said. "But not here." More Murgs gathered on the side of the street. It looked like we were the only game in town. "My shop is safe, and we should move quickly before Bellows returns. He does not like anyone touching his clock hands. Especially outsiders."

"We'll clean up his shop and meet you there," Fuzee said.

Strike left and headed to the other end of the village. I knew what she was going to do so I one-upped her by taking her hand and leading her to Bellows' shop. Once inside, we closed the sliding door with a *clang* and replaced the board. Most of the hands were back along the wall, but a few fell short, and we straightened out the rows, making sure the ones with burn marks were in the back. I was certain Bellows would understand.

We left through the back door as quickly as we came in. There was a grassy lane running behind the buildings, so we didn't have to wander the main drag and mingle with the Murgs. Just before we got to Strike's, Fuzee pulled me between two of the shops. It looked like a porch or patio, complete with a sturdy stone bench.

"Let's rest," she said. It seemed odd she would need a rest so close to Strike's shop, but I went along with it. We sat on the cool stone bench beneath an arch covered in blossoming flowers. I was in dire need of water, but it could wait until we got to Strike's.

Fuzee couldn't wait. She put her hands on my shoulders and pulled me in. I got about three inches from her face and had to turn away. This was just too weird. Fuzee was a girl, all right, at least mostly. I wanted to. I think. I just couldn't. She looked up at me with those mega-peepers, nearly in tears.

"I'm sorry," she said. "I just thought—"

"No, it's okay. Really. I'm just not ready for *that*."

Instead she stood, wrapped her short arms around me, and squeezed. I squeezed back. When she pulled away a few seconds later, hers eyes were spinning in crazy circles.

Superb.

CHAPTER SIXTEEN

It was back to business after that close call on the stone bench. Fuzee pulled me along the grassy trail until we came to the back of Strike's shop. We went around to use the front door, never saying a word to each other after the near-kiss.

There was still a lot of action on the main drag, with Murgs running here and there, some screaming at each other, while others just watched the activity. Some of these folks definitely looked like they needed to get outside more.

"Fluzee, CJ, come in, come in," Strike said from behind his counter. "Sit wherever you want." I laughed to myself because it sounded like "Seet vherever you vant" in his thick accent. I stopped in mid-giggle because I knew it was time to be serious.

There were only two chairs in the shop. Fuzee took the wooden chair, and I sat on a high stool that rocked slightly. I steadied myself and found it best to lean against the wall for support. Based on the decor, I figured Strike didn't get a whole lot of visitors.

I tried to swallow but only made a weird gulping noise. "Do you have any water, Strike? I'm pretty parched after that battle."

Strike's expression didn't change, but Fuzee gave me one of those looks that only girls can give. *All I did was ask for water*, I thought. Maybe that was a bad thing to do in Murg. Regardless, Strike went behind the curtain and returned seconds later with a small teacup filled halfway with water. At least I hoped it was water.

"It's the best I can do. Good water is scarce."

I thought about the stream we went through to get here. Seemed like plenty of water to me. I took a sip and it tasted just fine, so I polished off the rest and handed the teacup back to Strike. "Thanks. I needed that."

Strike returned to his spot as the commotion outside got louder. He didn't seem fazed by it one bit. "I know by your actions you have spoken with the Tick Tock Man. How does he plan to help us?"

I nearly slipped off my stool but caught myself. "He

doesn't. You guys started this mess, and you're going to have to fix it yourselves."

"Impossible," Strike said. "Out of the question."

I shook my head. "What is wrong with you people? If you don't do something, the Verge will run wild and no one will be able to stop them."

Strike leaned forward as far as he could. "The Kinzigs are completely unreasonable!" He smashed his fist down on the glass countertop. Somehow it managed not to shatter.

"That's what Fuzee said about you guys." I realized too late I probably shouldn't have brought that up. But I was getting tired of this runaround. It was time to change the subject. "What happened a hundred years ago? Albert, the Tick Tock Man, he said you've had a hundred years to fix the problem. So what gives?"

His eyes widened, and his head began to quiver. Then the keys and odd parts on the wall began to shake in unison. I thought for a second we were under attack, but Strike straightened, and the noise stopped. He silently left us and went behind the curtain. I could hear more knocking and clanging until Strike emerged with a large wooden box. He came out from behind the counter and began to take timepieces and various parts from the box and place them in a circle.

I knew an isochronal circle when I saw one. He took an odd-shaped part from the wall plus a normal clock from the wall behind me and completed the circle. I could have done the same thing in about half the time, but I didn't want him to know that. Albert had said isochronal circles were outlawed in Furtwangen, so I wanted to see what happened.

"There was peace for many years," he said. The circle parts began to rise and spin. "We were the happy little town of Furtwangen, and it was our calling to keep all the clocks in town working. It was a task we took quite seriously."

A birds-eye view of the town appeared in the circle. There was no pendulum wall between the two factions, just two distinct villages, each representing half of the town's clocks. There was some snow on the ground, giving it a Christmas card look.

"The more clocks there were, the happier we were," Strike continued. "The clockmakers in the village had an agreement with the clockmakers in town. There was never a problem."

The image in the circle changed to the building of the giant clock above the train station. Then to the one in Ripley Park. Then quickly through several others. I got the point.

"Through the years, we fixed the movements, replaced the hands, kept the gears oiled and running on time. We worked in groups, each assigned a specific timepiece. We were two villages working together, helping each other. It was a thing of beauty."

Now the images in the circle switched to the people of Hambleton. My people. They walked by the big clocks and pointed. A small child rocked back and forth in the same motion as a large pendulum. Folks dressed in old-fashioned clothes walked through Ripley Park and set their watches to the big clock near the fountain. The images looked so real.

I looked over at Fuzee, who was not even watching the circle. Her eyes were barely open. Something bad was going to be revealed, I could feel it.

"We had the best clocks in the entire state, maybe in the country," Strike said. "People came from everywhere to see them. Unfortunately, something strange started to happen. The Kinzigs became interested in their own clocks, and the good people of Murg stood by theirs. For years we shared everything, then parts became harder and harder to obtain from each other. A small group of workers began to operate out of the forest on the edge of both villages. They hoarded parts, demanded outrageous fees for their services. They called their town Enz."

"The Verge," I said. Gearheads immediately began to appear in the circle. They moved in groups, mostly, hassling villagers and causing trouble.

"That's right. Both villages had to make deals with members of the Verge to get certain parts. In return, the clocks would remain running. Both villages were happy with the arrangement, and nothing could stop us, except Mother Nature. With grave apologies to my friend Fluzee here, several clocks were hit by lightning and badly damaged. They managed to get the parts for the old Baptist church clock on the Murg side, but the other one … "

"The Urgos," I said. A quick peek at Fuzee showed her looking completely away from the circle as the clock exploded from the lightning bolt.

"That's right," Strike said. "Neither of us had the parts, and the Verge refused to help. Try as we might, we just couldn't save the Urgos."

"There are some," Fuzee said, "who swore there was a perfectly good mainspring in Murg, but they refused to give it up."

Strike focused his huge eyes in her direction, and she returned the gaze. The stare-down lasted a few seconds; Strike turned away with a little shake. "Yes. Some have said that. But it has never been proven."

"What happened to the Urgos?" I said, eager to keep the conversation moving.

"The tower is still there, but the town clockmaker had

to take out the movement, at least what was left of it. It's probably sitting on large shelf somewhere. A new clock was erected nearby several decades later, but that one did not need a representative."

I didn't need to look over at Fuzee. I could feel it. Losing your clock movement was apparently the worst thing that could happen to someone from Furtwangen. I glanced anyway, just in time to see her wipe tears from her massive eyes.

Another crash outside broke up our conversation, even though the circle remained. The noise died down within seconds, and Strike continued his talk.

"The pendulum makers decided to separate the two villages for our own good. The giant pendulums have been there ever since. Everyone knows there are ways to get around them, but they are a stark reminder that these two villages remain at odds." The swinging pendulums appeared in the circle, their brass bobs gleaming as they swung. "It was about this time that one of the Kinzig leaders figured out how to create an isochronal circle, much like this one."

"We were always told they were from Murg," Fuzee added.

"Regardless," Strike said, "the circles were fairly harmless at first, timepieces synchronized in such a way to view the past. The leaders then discovered that if enough mainsprings are in it, the circle can be used to move from place to place and time to time. It was utter chaos. Two venturesome souls tried to go back and save the Urgos from its ultimate fate, but they were unsuccessful." He paused for a moment for his unique version of a sigh. "And they never returned."

The images stopped, and the room grew darker. I remembered what Albert said about abusing the use of the circle, but I hadn't realized it ended tragically. Strike looked ready to quit, but there was still something I needed to know. "So what you're saying is that using the isochronal circles to go anywhere was outlawed, right?"

Strike took a small key from the counter and stood near the circling objects. With a flick, he tossed the key toward the center of the circle, and it bounced off with a spark. "The power to use them for that reason was removed from both villages by the master clockmaker, the one known as the Tick Tock Man. Now only those who are able to venture between worlds can make them work."

"You mean spandrels, right?" I asked.

"I believe that is the name, yes."

The timepieces and parts dropped harmlessly to the floor, and Strike began to pick them up. He was muttering something I couldn't make out as he placed the parts in the box.

The disturbance outside grew louder. A high-pitched grinding cut through everything and forced Fuzee and Strike to cover their sensitive ears. I went for the door and peeked out. The grinding stopped, and I saw people at the other end of the main street running away from a giant gear over two stories tall as it made its way along, grinding up anything in its path. It looked like the Verge were back with a vengeance. She took my hand and led me a little farther out to get a better view.

"We have to stop it," I said.

"How?"

"I don't know. Maybe if we combine our strength—"

The door to Strike's shop slammed, followed by several thumps and bangs and assorted other noises. Fuzee tried the door, but it wouldn't budge. "Strike!"

We heard glass shatter, more than likely from the counters, followed by some yelling. Fuzee threw herself against the door, but it wouldn't budge. Then she backed up, started spinning and ground a hole in the door. I followed her through. The place was a mess.

"Strike?" she yelled.

The curtain behind the counter had been ripped off, and we hurried into the back room. She kept yelling his name, but no one responded. The back door was open, and we ran into the daylight. Three members of the Verge carried Strike high above them as he struggled to get free. A fourth gearhead stopped and looked right us as he snapped the straps of his overall. His gear head spun fast, then slow, like he was revving an engine.

"Strike!" Fuzee yelled, but it was too late as they disappeared into the hedgerow.

CHAPTER SEVENTEEN

"We have to save him," Fuzee said. She started to follow, but I held her back. "What are you doing?"

"We can't go after Strike yet. That's what they want."

She pulled my arm, but I held firm, even knowing full well she probably could have ripped my arm off if she wanted to. "How do you know what they want? You're not from here."

"That's right, I'm not. But you said it yourself. They live on fear. In my world this happens all the time, and we call them terrorists. Fear causes confusion, and confusion leads to bad choices. We'll find him when the time is right, just like we'll find Ratchet. Trust me."

I never asked her to trust me before, but she took a

step my way, which was a good sign. I was getting better at reading her body language and facial expressions. Her eyes spun but only for a few seconds. She was thinking about it. Maybe "taking it under advisement," as one of my teachers used to say.

"We have to get back to Kinzig," she said. This time she didn't ask as she pulled me back through Strike's shop.

"What about the attack? We have to help the Murg—"

"They won't need our help. Trust me on this one."

"But—"

"Look!" She led me out the front door in time to see the giant attacking gear topple over on its side. The good people of Murg went after it with long poles, shafts, and various other parts. Several members of Verge were on the business end of the attacks too. "Once they see how something is done, they never forget."

Several Murgs were on the rooftops throwing parts and other debris down on the Verge. It appeared to be working, as the gearheads gave up and headed out of town. The normally quiet Murgs were whooping it up and cheering. Well, at least a few of them were.

"If we head back through the ogive," Fuzee said, "we might be able to return without too much trouble."

"Or we can walk straight there." I pointed in the general

direction of Kinzig. On the horizon was the giant wall of pendulums that separated the two villages.

"The two of us have no shot against the giant pendulums. They'll slice us to bits." She winced at the thought of it.

"Not today they won't, thanks to the gearheads."

"What do you mean?"

"That giant gear they left. If we can get it close enough to the pendulums, I'll bet our combined powers can find a way to knock them out."

To demonstrate, I summoned a small gear, no more than four inches across, off the street and made it spin. With the zing of my finger, I directed it toward a flowerpot in front of a number-making shop. The gear buzzed through the pot and shattered it, sending dirt flying everywhere.

"So all we have to do is carry the giant brass gear to the boundary and bust through it, right? No problem. You just grab one side, and I'll grab the other—"

"Not us. Them." I pointed to the Murgs who milled about the area admiring their handiwork. "If we can get them to move it, I think you and I can do the rest."

Her eyes spun just a little. "I don't know. It's just that—"

"Just what? Just that they're Murgs and you're not. We have to bring down that wall or the Verge will be back tomorrow and the next day and the next. They want the two villages to hate each other so they can be in control." I found two more gears on the ground and sent them flying into two flowerpots, destroying them easily. "This has to end right now." Another gear and another flowerpot destroyed.

Her nodding started slowly, then became very animated. It was an emotion I had never seen from her, like she was channeling Strike or something. "It might just work. Now we just have to convince the Murgs to give us a hand."

"I'll try," I said. "After all, I'm probably some sort of hero around these parts."

She put her hand up. "No. I'll talk to them. You're still an outsider, in spite of your heroics. Besides, I speak their language." She kept her hand up and started walking. "Just wait here and let me handle this."

I did as Fuzee asked and watched as she gathered some of the Murgs and brought them to the giant gear, still leaning against the side of a building. As she spoke, more and more joined the meeting. She motioned my way a few times, then made a spinning motion in the air. She used her arm to act like a pendulum, and then flew an imaginary gear into it. This stunned a few onlookers, but it seemed to be working. One by one they nodded in agreement; then the Murgs left to form their own strategy session as Fuzee returned, all smiles.

"They'll do it. We need to give them a few minutes to

gather supplies and enough folks to carry it, but they are all in."

"That Fuzee charm strikes again."

The Murgs went right to work making a platform strong enough to carry the gear. Most of them were not too big, so it would take every available body to move it. The side door of one of the shops opened, and workers carried out three large metal rings of increasing size, maybe five, ten, and fifteen feet in diameter. They attached them together, starting with the smallest in the middle and working out. They quickly pounded and bolted and even welded a few areas. They added arms coming out from the largest ring until it looked a captain's wheel on a boat.

Next, some nimble types got on the roof and attached a rope to the top of the gear. The others pulled until the giant gear landed on top of the wheel with a *clang*. A few adjustments later, they were ready to go.

"Come on." She took my hand and led me along. "Looks like they saved two spots for us."

Sure enough, there were two spokes left, so we each grabbed a handle. On the count of three, we lifted the massive gear in the air and steadied it. A few of the lighter and odd-shaped Murgs fell down, but they all scrambled up and took their spots.

The walk was slow and unsteady at first, but we worked as a team, and soon it became pretty easy. We cleared the edge of town and came to a meadow. The grass was tall and the ground uneven, but we managed not to drop the gear as we pressed on. No one complained or gave orders or any of that stuff. They seemed to know exactly where to go.

Then came the bog. It seemed like just another grassy area, but we all started to sink in the grass/mud mixture. The gear stayed on the wheel, hovering just a foot or so from the surface. We were truly stuck.

A voice from the front shouted, "Form a line!" Murgs began to dislodge themselves from the boggy mess and move to the front while the rest of held steady. Just enough moved up and just enough stayed behind, like they'd done it every day. The wheel was passed forward a few feet at a time, and Fuzee and I even got our chance to join in the rotation. After about twenty feet, the ground got firm, so we all took our own spokes. It was a short jaunt to the boundary, and we stopped in the shadow of the giant pendulums to rest. Murgs took to the ground to catch their breath and soothe their sore muscles—if they had muscles. It was time for Fuzee and me to take over.

We walked to the edge of the giant pendulums and observed the pattern. They came in all sizes, and there was never more than a second of empty space between them. The edges of the bobs were as sharp as razorblades.

"I say we go after the tall one," she said, pointing just to our right. "If we can take that one down, the others will fall."

"We'll be trying to hit a moving target, so it won't be easy," I added.

"You just get it airborne, and we'll see what happens."

By now the Murgs were starting to get curious about the battle plan. Fuzee went over and talked to a few of them, using her hands to illustrate the attack. Most nodded, although it was hard to tell with the ones who had odd-shaped heads. They all got the message, though, and backed away.

It was my turn to focus on the task at hand. I hadn't had this power long, but I could feel it welling up inside me. I kept my back to the giant gear and paced off twenty steps. I turned quickly and put my arm straight out with the palm facing up.

Rise.

I commanded the gear to lift from the wheel. It wavered and shook and even squeaked a few times, but it remained on its platform.

Deep breath. Deep breath. *Focus.*

Rise.

The gear lifted a foot off the platform, and several Murgs gasped.

Keep focusing.

The gear went up to five feet, then ten, then twenty. I could feel it completely under my control and leveled it off to the height we needed. The gear was too heavy for me to both lift and spin, so it was Fuzee's turn to spring into action.

"Ready?" she asked.

I broke my gaze and nodded in her direction. "Ready."

She rose and spun like I had never seen her spin. She backed away from the gear, then slowly made her way toward it. They met with a spark, and the gear started turning. It took all my strength to keep it steady while she increased the revolutions.

It was finally time for the attack. While she whirled, I moved the gear closer and closer to the tallest pendulum. Sparks flew as the gear ground away at the swinging arm. There was a slight bounce, but Fuzee and I kept it steady, and the sparks continued to fly. The pendulum stopped swinging, and I gave the gear one last push, finally cutting through.

I believe what happened next is called the "domino effect." She pulled away, and the gear slowed down. When it was safe, I lowered the gear to the ground. The longest pendulum broke away and disrupted the next one and the next one until they all clanged into one another and stopped swinging. In an instant the entire wall of pendulums came tumbling down.

The Murgs went crazy, whooping it up and hugging each other. Fuzee, still frazzled from her encounter, joined in and gave me a solid hug too. "You did it!" she yelled. "You destroyed the pendulums."

"We did it." I made a circular motion with my hand while the Murgs continued their celebration. "It was a total team effort."

CHAPTER EIGHTEEN

A very tall, spring-shaped Murg came over and patted both of us on the shoulder. "Thank you, EJ," he said in a squeaky voice. "And Fuzee too." Besides Strike, this guy was the only Murg I'd heard utter a peep, even if he did mess up my name.

"Ding dong, the witch is dead," I said. The spring-shaped guy didn't have crazy, spinning eyes like Fuzee, but I could tell neither one knew what that meant. I guess *The Wizard of Oz* never made it to Furtwangen.

The Murgs were having a great time with the toppled pendulums, throwing them as far as they could into the bog and meadow, and even to the Kinzig side. Speaking of Kinzig, several of their villagers came over to see what happened.

They lined the now make-believe boundary and watched as pendulums flew. A few brave ones picked up their own and gave them a chuck, like it was a contest. Maybe it was.

"We should go now," I said.

"I agree," Fuzee said. "I think something great is about to happen here, but we need to get to Kinzig."

We crossed the barrier, carefully avoiding the sharp edges of the downed pendulums. By now the villagers from both sides were sharing stories, their wild body language helping to set the scenes. A group removed pendulums from a high spot near the middle of the boundary and created a clearing. Murgs moved freely into Kinzig and vice versa. It made me proud to witness it.

We arrived in Kinzig a few minutes later and found the scene similar to the one in Murg. From the looks of it, the Verge made a battering ram from several large chimes tied together and with gears for wheels. A few buildings were damaged, but the battering ram was toppled on its side. Several villagers were on it, whacking away with large hammers and various other tools. There was not a gearhead in sight.

"Bad day for the Verge," I said. "They got their butts kicked twice."

Villagers returned with some of the smaller pendulums

and began striking the battering ram with them. The brass-on-brass contact sent sparks in all directions. The chimes took a pounding and soon were flattened. This led to even wilder cheering from the onlookers. They were definitely getting the hang of retaliation.

"The gearheads'll be back," Fuzee said. "It's what they do."

Some members of the group huddled and began to sing.

"Not if they know what's good for 'em," I said.

Several Murgs joined the Kinzigs in the celebration. I used to think they all looked alike, but now I could see that the Murgs walked and moved differently. If I took the time to really observe, the difference was there to see.

"We're here," Fuzee said, with an elbow to my ribs. I guess I had spaced out there a moment.

"Where's 'here'?" I asked.

"It's Hammer's shop. He's a good friend of mind."

"How good?" I realized my question had a hint of jealousy to it. I hoped she didn't pick up on it.

"He represents the Rombach. It has been around for over a hundred years, thanks to his expertise."

"The Rombach? I've never heard of it, before."

Her eyes did the spin cycle; then she nodded. "You may know it as the movement for the Methodist church."

That would make it the five o'clock position on the giant

town clock face. Two numbers away from where Fuzee used to be. "So what can this Hammer guy do for us?"

"He has some items we can take with us to Enz. It will make our lives a lot easier."

"What kind of items?"

"You'll see."

We entered the shop and took a quick look around. It looked similar to Strike's, except the walls were covered with small gears. There was a commotion in the back room, followed by silence.

"Hammer?" Fuzee said. "Hammer, are you here?"

We waited ten, twenty, thirty seconds; then she led the way through the hallway to the back. The place was a mess. The walls had large gouges cut into them, and parts were scattered all over the place. I heard a whimpering sound coming from a small closet, so I opened it. Inside was a Kinzig shaped like a thin, metal tube. He appeared to be was sobbing as he peeked out at us.

"Arbor? It's me, Fuzee. You can come out now. It's safe."

Arbor looked at me and turned away. The sobbing continued. I took the hint and moved out of sight. With a little more coaxing, she convinced Arbor to leave the closet. They had a private conversation at the other end of the hall. I was content to watch from my end. Arbor was very animated, cutting throughout the air at vicious angles with his tiny hands before sobbing some more. Fuzee tried to console him, and it appeared to be working. She motioned me back to the front room, and I met her there a minute later. I knew what she was going to say.

"The Verge," she said, with more anger than I'd ever heard. "They took Hammer during the last attack."

"What are the items you were talking about? Are they still here?"

She scanned the room. "Yes. Hammer and Arbor make the finest pinions in the land. They will come in handy when we meet up with the Verge." She tossed a small sack in my direction. "Arbor said it's okay to take as many as we need, so fill the sack, and maybe your pockets too. Trust me; these are handy items to have around."

I still didn't know all my clock parts as well as Fuzee and the others, but I did know that pinions are the small gears that turn the bigger gears. Each tooth is called a leaf. I did as she asked and grabbed as many as I could. They were made of hardened steel, and I was already picturing ways to use them in battle against the gearheads. I slung the pinion-stuffed bag over my shoulder and followed Fuzee out the front. The crushed remains of the battering ram were still in the middle of the road, but no one was paying attention to it any more.

"So what's the fastest way to Enz?" I asked, as we walked out of town.

"If we use the Sequence, we can be there in a snap. But I'm pretty sure it's heavily guarded, so we should go through the ogive again."

I figured as much, but I wanted to make sure. We took the same path as before toward the ogive. The path Fuzee cut through the bush was still there but was starting to fill in. They had some fast-growing vegetation here in Kinzig.

"So what can we expect in Enz?" I asked, as we trudged along the trail.

"I've never actually been there," she said. "I've only heard the stories. Strike told me the entire village is up against a hillside so they can see strangers coming. That doesn't surprise me."

We came to the large group of trees and quickly stepped around them. "Any idea where Strike and Ratchet are being held?"

"Nope. We'll just have to adjust to the circumstances when we get there."

Adjust to the circumstances? She was speaking like some sort of warrior goddess. Hey, maybe she was.

We entered the ogive, and this time the stream was running faster. I wasn't concerned about getting wet, and

Fuzee didn't seem to be either, so we trudged through the shin-deep water with only her glowing eyes to guide us. It seemed to take us twice as long as the previous time.

"Stay left," she said. I followed her toward the wall, where the water was only ankle-deep. We had to duck to avoid the curve of the arched ceiling, but neither of us was very tall, so no big deal. I remembered this section from before, when it was just sand and rocks, and it began to worry me. The rushing water was much louder than before.

There was an unmistakable sound of splashing just ahead of us, and I backed against the wall. Something jumped on my head, and I tossed it off with a scream. A muskrat. It looked like a giant, wet rat as it swam away.

Fuzee was up ahead a few paces and turned my way, lighting the water in front of me. The stupid muskrats were everywhere.

"What do they want?" I asked.

"Nothing. They're just friendly. I told you they're fairly harmless. Nothing will happen if we keep moving."

That wasn't the reassuring answer I was looking for, but I trudged on.

"Faster," she said as she took my hand. The water got deeper and the muskrats more plentiful as they bumped into our knees as we waded through. They didn't grab or bite.

They just bumped. It was hard to do anything about them in the deep water. Finally, I could see the split ahead. Left went to Murg, right went to Enz. We rested on a shallow sandbar just before the split. The muskrats continued crawling along the ledge that ran the course of the tunnel and a few started to crawl up my legs. I kicked as many as I could and sent them flying across the water.

The majority of the rushing water was coming from the right. Just our luck. Fuzee's eyes lit up the right channel, revealing nothing but water and muskrats. Great.

We entered the channel. "Stay close," she said. There did not appear to be a shallow part or a sandbar, plus the smell was much worse than last time. After some fifty feet, the channel bent slightly to the right. We could finally see the light at the end and even some coming from above. Fortunately, there were no muskrats. In fact, it got eerily quiet except for the sound of water. Fuzee stopped, and I nearly bumped into her.

"Do you hear that?" she asked.

"What?"

I turned to see the dim light behind us suddenly disappear. Then the light at the end went away too. The stream turned to a trickle, and we stood in a bed of silt and rocks. Her eyes shot in every direction, casting short bursts of light all over the tunnel.

"There it is again," she said. I heard it too. The grinding sound started low, but soon filled the tunnel. The sour smell came next, and I knew were in the company of the Verge.

"Not good," Fuzee said softly. "Not good at all."

Gearheads filled both ends of the tunnel, and we were completely surrounded.

CHAPTER NINETEEN

We were in total darkness, except for the glow of Fuzee's eyes and a small patch of light poking in from the ceiling. I couldn't tell how many gearheads were there with us, but based on sound and smell alone, we were way outnumbered.

"Now what?" I asked in a hushed voice. I wasn't sure why I was whispering under these circumstances.

"It's time to use the pinions," she said. "Open your bag."

I took the bag off my shoulder, set it down between us, and pulled open the drawstring. "How do they work?"

"Pinions turn gears. The gearheads may fend off a few, but if you keep them coming, it will buy me enough time to get us out up there." She motioned to the light coming from above. It didn't seem like much, but I trusted she could do it.

The gearheads were closing in, so we had no choice.

"On the count of three," she said. "One … two … three."

We both began flinging pinions toward the gearheads. With a flick of my wrist, I made them spin as they approached their targets. Some caromed off and landed on the walls or in the water. A few found their marks as gearheads began spinning wildly, bouncing off the others and skittering from side to side. I used both hands, one for each end. I alternated tossing the pinions with making them spin, and I got on quite a roll. Sparks flew as the gearheads tried to avoid the pinions. She was right. Those little buggers knew just what to do.

While I kept the gearheads away, Fuzee moved to the other side of the now-dry creek bed. She kept looking up as she continued to fling her remaining pinions right and left.

"Found it," she said. "Grab your pinions and follow me."

I sent out two more pinions, cinched the bag, and hoisted it on my shoulder. I ran quickly to the other side of the creek bed as she positioned herself under a tiny beam of light.

She pointed straight up and nodded. "On the count of three, I'm going to invert. Grab my hands and hold on. One … two … three."

She began to spin rapidly and turned herself upside down, so her pointy lower body was aiming up. Her arms dangled, and I locked my wrists around hers. Then up we went.

I'm not sure what the top of the tunnel was made of, but it rained down on me as Fuzee's torso ground through it. I closed my eyes and held on tight until we reached daylight. We fell to the soft ground, and I shook out the dirt and dust and who knows what else in my hair.

Fuzee was already prepared to move on. "Time to give our friends a drink." I followed her through the thicket until we came to the spot where the creek was dammed with rock and chunks of earth. "They knew we were coming and increased the flow once we were inside the ogive to slow us down. Then they blocked it off completely to trap us."

"So what do you have in mind?"

"Start moving rocks." She began lifting some large boulders and tossing them aside. I couldn't budge anything but small ones using just my muscles. It was time to use my other skill. I put my finger out and commanded a bowling ball-size rock to lift. It twitched, then wobbled, then lifted about a foot. I moved it over and out of the way with just flick. We worked in tandem, moving as many rocks as we could. In just a few seconds, water began to pour over the shortened dam; then the whole thing gave way as a giant wave roared down the tunnel.

"I have to see this," Fuzee said. She took off toward the ogive. We soon came to dense brush, and she spun through it like it was spaghetti. We came to a short cliff that overlooked

Kinzig. Below us were the ogive and the stream barely flowing out of it. Then we heard screams and grinding as the wave flushed all the gearheads out into the woods. They struggled to avoid sinking or smashing into rocks and trees, but most were unsuccessful. It was fabulous.

"I've seen enough," Fuzee said. "Time to find our friends." She could not contain her smile.

We arrived at the edge of Enz knowing there were a lot fewer members of the Verge to worry about. I still had a good number of pinions left in my bag and a few in my pockets. That voice in my head told me I'd probably be needing them. *That's okay,* I thought. I have a gearhead's worst nightmare standing next to me. Oh yeah, and I was getting pretty good at this too.

Enz was not so much a village like Kinzig or Murg, but more of a campground. The main road—call it a path—was lined with tents and lean-tos and various structures made from scrap. These gearheads were certainly not house-proud.

"They're not big into anything with walls," she said. "So no need to worry about Strike and Hammer and Ratchet being held underground or in an attic."

"How do we find them?" I asked.

"I can find Strike easy enough. He is a keymaster, and we have our own secret tone. If I start and he hears it, he'll finish.

It's something a lot of us can do as a means of long- or short-range communication."

It had just dawned on me that I hadn't seen a single telephone or other electronic device anywhere in Furtwangen. I guess secret tones were the way to go.

"Won't sending out a tone give us away?" I asked.

"No. At least not immediately. Tones are a common sound, so even the gearheads are used to hearing them on a daily basis. You probably didn't notice, but I've heard at least three since we got here."

She was right about me not noticing. I guess I had just gotten used to the sounds around there.

"Here's what I'm going to do. See that clump of trees over there? I'm going to send the keymaster's tone; then we'll relocate. If Strike answers, we'll keep moving closer until we can pin the position down. Got it?"

"Got it."

"And keep those pinions handy in case we run into some curious friends."

She moved into the open and pulled out a small metal hammer from the shoulder region of her cone-shaped body. She struck herself in three different parts of her body, sending out sort of a *bing-bung-bong* sound. We ran quickly to the clump of trees and listened. The response was faint, but I could hear a *bung-bong-bing* tone.

"That's Strike. I'm sure of it. He must be on the far end of the road." Two smaller gearheads heard the tone and came out to look around. They wandered along the road for just a minute or so, then disappeared into a ragged-looking tent.

I pointed to a large boulder some hundred feet up the road. "How about there?"

Fuzee nodded, and we sprinted for the boulder. A quick peek assured me no one saw us. She took her hammer and sent out another three-part tone. Strike answered within five seconds. "There," she said, pointing to a rustic old building across and up the road. "Strike is in the back. Hammer and Ratchet are with him."

It was strange, but I could sense the presence of Ratchet too. We had no secret tone or other normal means of communication. I just felt it. The thought of it made me smile. "So how do we get them out?" I asked.

She pulled me down and out of sight as three gearheads came running by. They stopped just ahead of the rock, looked around, and then continued on.

"We'll have to split up. It's too quiet around here, which makes me think they're out on patrols or hatching up something else. Plus, some of them will recover from the river ride and return."

"Why don't we just rush in and get them if no one's around?"

Her eyes spun for a few seconds and stopped at the same time. "It doesn't seem right. We need to split up to make this work."

I looked to the small hill behind us. Partway up was a thicket just big enough to hide in. It was perfect. "I'll take care of the ones coming back from up there, and you take care of getting the others out. Is that what you were thinking?"

She nodded. "Like you read my mind." She took the hammer and sent out a different tone, this time a sequence of four parts. "I just let Strike know I'm coming for him." She pulled me close and got right up in my face. "Be careful."

"I will." Her eyes met mine, and I felt a huge lump in my throat, like I had a Skittle stuck in there. Something about her was different, almost like she was more human than before. I knew right then I would do anything for her.

I let go and scrambled up to my position. I could see most of Enz from there without much trouble. I watched as Fuzee moved from the rock to a spot behind a shed that was falling apart. She looked at me and nodded, then flashed her eyes. She was across the path, next to Strike's building.

I turned to my right just in time to see a half-dozen gearheads returning, and they did not look happy.

It was showtime.

CHAPTER TWENTY

Wet and angry was the best way to describe the small mob that made its way toward the center of Enz. Many of them spun in one direction, then the other, to dry off their massive gears. Metal parts and water were never a good mix.

A quick look across the street showed that Fuzee had disappeared around the back of the structure where Strike, Hammer, and Ratchet were being held. I figured it was my time to slow down the intruding gearheads. The good thing about being on a hillside was having gravity in my favor. The hill was strewn with fairly round boulders the size of bowling balls. From my hiding spot, I commanded the first boulder to lift just a little. The slope of the hill did the rest, sending the rolling boulder in a beeline toward the gearheads. The ones closest to the hill saw it coming and moved aside, but one unlucky gearhead in the back was not paying attention and took the full force of the boulder, which knocked him back a good five feet.

I started several more rocks rolling, but I knew the gearheads would be able to dodge the boulders unless I added something else to the mix. I opened my bag of pinions and sent them flying toward the gang. As before, most pinions missed their mark, but the gearheads were so concerned with the pinions, they forgot about the boulders, and half were toppled. Some of the others were spun temporarily by the pinion. I kept the rock and pinion barrage going for as long as I could. I checked on Fuzee and didn't see her, so I could only hope she found a way in.

The unmistakable smell of the Verge filled my nostrils. I turned and saw that the cliff above me was lined with gearheads. The grinding noise soon followed. I reached into my pinion bag, but it was almost empty. More gearheads arrived to my right and to my left. Where had they all come from? I had no choice but to book it into town, so I jumped out of the thicket and ran as fast as I could toward Enz. Fuzee came out of the structure she had been casing, with Strike, Ratchet, and Hammer right behind her.

We met along the path, and Ratchet wrapped his long arms around me. I could feel his chest heaving as he squeezed me hard. "Are you okay, Carlton?" he asked, as he gave me a good looking-over.

"I'm okay. What about you? Did they hurt you?" His hair was messed up, and his clothes were torn, so I already knew the answer.

"Don't worry about me. Let's just get out of here."

But another look around revealed the startling truth. It was a trap, and we were completely surrounded by the Verge. They came out of the shacks and tents and from behind trees. This had all been too easy.

"We are in deep trouble," Ratchet said. "I never should have brought you here."

We instinctively formed a circle with our backs to the center. I tried to move a few of them, but there were too way many. The pungent smell was worse than ever, so I had to take shallow breaths to keep from gagging. Fuzee grabbed my hand and held it tight. I thought for a moment she would rise above us and save herself, but she stayed. We would go down together.

A few of the larger gearheads began spinning like buzz saws while the others whooped and hollered. It was just a matter of time before we would be chopped to pieces.

They moved closer, and then stopped. Their gear-shaped heads jerked up, like they were listening for something.

Then it came. A high-pitched swishing sound like no other I'd ever heard. The gearheads looked confused, and then began to back away. Once they parted, I could see the source of the sound. The villagers had arrived, and they brought the pendulums with them. They had built machines from gears and posts and springs and various other parts and used them to twirl the pendulums like whirlybirds. Some twirled just one; others up to three, maybe four at a time. The razor-sharp pendulums ripped into the ragtag buildings, easily destroying them.

"It's Arbor," Fuzee said, pointing to one of the larger devices. "Kinzig has arrived."

"Murg too," I said, gesturing to a familiar group.

The villagers drove, pushed, and pulled their pendulum machines all over Enz and knocked down everything in their path. The five of us moved behind a rock formation and watched from relative safety. The Kinzigs and Murgs chased the Verge members up the hills, down the paths, and even knocked a few trees down to get them. In a matter of minutes, Enz was nothing but dust and rubble.

"We need to leave," Ratchet said to me. "I'm pretty sure our work is done here."

I motioned to the crowd gathered along the path. They were cheering and patting each other on the back. "What about them?"

"It looks like they figured it out. It only took them a hundred years."

"Ratchet is right," Fuzee said. "You can't stay any longer. I'll take you back."

Strike and Hammer left us and joined the others in celebration. We didn't get so much as a thanks from either one, but that was no surprise. Nor was it necessary.

Fuzee started up the path, away from the festivities. "We'll go this way," she said. "But keep your guard up because gearheads may still be lurking."

Ratchet and I followed her along the grassy trail. No matter how hard I tried to catch up, she kept her distance. Ratchet nodded and put his arm out to slow me down. We settled in a good twenty feet behind her. "You learned a few things. I was watching from a small window where they were holding us. What you did with those pinions was amazing."

"It was the Tick Tock Man. After I came back from visiting him, I … well, I just knew how."

"Albert is very wise. Perhaps the wisest person I've ever met. What did he tell you?"

We increased speed just to keep the same distance from

Fuzee. I wasn't sure where we were going, but it wouldn't take long to get there at this pace.

"He told me the history behind the two feuding villages and how he stopped the clocks until they resolved it." I turned and looked behind us as the celebration continued. "I think they just did."

"Sure looks that way. Now all we have to do is get the mainspring back. Then these folks can return to the business of keeping the clocks running."

A short path to our right took us into the Sequence, and Fuzee kept up the pace as we moved along the catwalk. I stopped trying to catch her. Finally, we came to a large movement, and we ducked under the gears and center posts. She faced us for the first time since we left. Her cheeks were flushed, and her eyes didn't have their usual spark. If I didn't know any better, I'd say she had been crying.

"You can go back this way," she said with a nod toward the clock face. Then she looked away. Why was she ignoring me?

"I can't believe this is over," I said, hoping to spark something in her. "So what's going to happen now?"

She continued to look the other way. I was about ready to head toward the clock face and leave when she spun around and got nose to nose with me. "I'll tell you what's going to happen, *Carlton*. You and your friend will go back to your quiet little town and return to your lives. We here in Furtwangen will get the clocks running again, but hey, that's what we do, right? We keep your clocks running like, well, like clockwork."

I couldn't help but wonder if all girls were this weird. I mean, we fought side by side for the entire battle, and now this? I decided to try another approach. "Come with us," I said. "You'll love it on the other side."

"I can't. I've told you that already. I don't represent anymore. I'm just Fuzee. All I'll ever be is Fuzee."

I put my arms out to hold her.

"Don't!"

"Whatever you're going to do," Ratchet said, "make it snappy, because we have to get back. I'll be over there." He motioned behind the big cogwheel.

Fuzee and I stood silently for what seemed like minutes. I didn't dare make a move toward her, so I paced. I had to think of something to say. Anything. "That was the most fun I've had in my life. I'm going to miss you. A lot."

She turned completely away from me, and this time I knew she was crying. Great. Way to blow the last goodbye. She wanted to kiss me before, but I wouldn't let her. I could tell by her look she wanted to again. I think I wanted to, but something held me back. Was she a machine or just a girl?

"Well, I should be going," I said, with a turn toward the clock face.

I never made it. She pulled me around and took me by both hands. Her cone-shaped body began to spin, and we rose up off the catwalk until we were six feet above it. We hovered, then came slowly down. Before landing, she gave me a peck on the cheek. When she was done, my legs felt wobbly.

"Goodbye, CJ. Be well."

She went to the catwalk and waited. Ratchet gently pulled me by the arm. "It's time to go. Now."

When I turned back, she was gone.

CHAPTER TWENTY-ONE

Ratchet had to practically drag me to the exit area, but we made it there. It wasn't long before we were using our watches to return to the old Baptist church.

"Sorry to rush you," Ratchet said. We scurried along the sidewalk in front of the old church. "Time is of the essence."

"Where are we going?"

"To see Albert, the Tick Tock Man."

"Why?"

"He has the Hoffhalder. I'll explain when we get there. Come on; let's run!"

He took off running, and I sprinted to catch up. None of this made any sense, especially the running part. "Don't you have a car?" I struggled to get the words out. "Grown-ups drive cars, right?"

"It's still near your house, remember? Besides, it's only four blocks."

He moved pretty well for an old guy, easily keeping up with my young legs. Three blocks later we turned the corner and came to Barron Road. The Clock Shop was just ahead. We slowed down and began to walk, thankfully. As I caught my breath I thought of something Ratchet told me earlier in the day.

"Wait a minute. Why did you make me find Albert when you knew all along where he was?"

"It was important you seek him out. It's part of the process."

"What process?"

We finally came to The Clock Shop at 33 Barron Road. Ratchet opened the squeaky door. "You'll see." He shooed me up the stairs. "Let's go."

I arrived at the top first and opened the door to the shop. It looked just as it did during my last visit. All the clocks seemed to tick in sync. All pendulums swung the same way. It was eerie.

Adele appeared from a back room, holding a tissue to her eyes.

"We're too late, aren't we?" Ratchet asked.

"I'm afraid so," she said, dabbing her right eye. "The paramedics came, but there was nothing they could do. He's gone."

"I'm so sorry, Adele. He was a great man, and a great clockmaker. The best I've ever seen."

She blew loudly into her tissue. "Thank you. Yes. Yes, he was." Then another honk.

I waved my hands out in front of them. This was happening all so fast. "Wait a minute. You're telling me the Tick Tock Man is dead? That just can't be true. I-I saw him earlier today, and he seemed just fine."

"He has been quite ill," Adele said. "He hung on just long enough to return the mainspring."

"So that means the clocks in town are back up and running, right?" I asked.

"Did he complete the pivot?" Ratchet asked.

"He did," Adele said. She was no longer crying or blowing her nose, making it easier to understand the words, although I didn't know what they meant by "pivot."

Finally, a smile came to her face as she nodded. "It was a wonderful experience, CJ—I mean Carlton. You'll be great."

Wait. How did my name get into this? Ratchet slapped me on the back nearly as hard as Fuzee used to.

"Congratulations, kid. Out with the old and in with the

new. What a glorious day!"

It seemed like both of them had gone completely nuts and weren't making any sense. I backed away from the counter. "Okay, what's going on?"

"You didn't tell him?" Adele said.

"Tell me what?" I looked at both and neither returned the gaze.

"You are the new Tick Tock Man. Albert chose you before his clock struck midnight. He completed the pivot, which is the transition of all his power and knowledge."

"But why me?"

"Albert had no children," Adele said. "So he was free to choose. You probably didn't realize it during your visit."

That would explain why I could make things move, just like Albert did during my visit. But still, I was no clock expert. Or was I? Suddenly, my head felt like a clockopedia.

"Carlton," Ratchet said, "what is the main gear train of a timepiece?"

"A going train."

"Very good. Now what is the reduction gear train that turns a clock's hands?"

I knew that one too. "The motion work."

He quizzed me on a dozen more clock-related questions and somehow, I got them all right. I could feel the clocks in the rooms like never before. The tall grandfather clock's tick was different from the others. The small wall clock above it had its own sound. They came at me from everywhere, and I took it all in.

Then a strange feeling came over me, like I had experienced a damaged clock. There was just enough of it left to speak to me. It was in the back. It was all alone. It needed my help.

It was the Urgos. Or what was left of the Urgos.

"Are you all right?' Adele asked, as I tried to listen for the Urgos.

"Yeah," Ratchet added. "You look kind of scary."

I snapped my fingers a few times. "Many years ago the Urgos was damaged by lightning, remember?"

"That was before my time," Ratchet said. "But, yes, I've heard of it. Why?

"Its movement is still in this building. I can feel it."

"That's not possible," Adele said. "I know every clock and part in here."

"It's here. I'll take you to it."

I jumped over the counter with a quick swing of my legs. Ratchet prepared to jump too but crawled over instead. I listened for the Urgos and led the others to a small room on the left. Adele opened the door and turned on the light.

"It's just cleaning supplies in here," she said, sweeping

her hand across the room. "And various other chemicals we use on clock parts. Albert liked to keep them separate from everything else."

I pointed to a cabinet in the upper corner. "In there."

Adele tugged on the handle, but it was locked. "I'm pretty sure we only keep old coffee pots up here. Now where is that key?"

"I'll get it open," I said. Adele backed away, and I slid open all the drawers with a flick of my wrist. A few keys flew up and hovered at eye level. Most were the wrong size, and they fell back in their drawers. Two remained. I sent the first into the lock and twisted it. No luck. I sent the second in, and the cabinet opened with a click. Adele swung the door open.

"See? Just coffee pots and such." She took them down one at time and placed them on the counter below. "There's nothing else here."

But there was something else. "There's a slider door in the back of the cabinet. Open it, please."

Adele stood on the counter and reached into the cabinet. "There's no—" Her hand touched the back wall, and it began to slide, revealing a void. "I don't believe it." She pulled out a large wooden box and placed it on the counter. I popped open the top and there it was. The Urgos. Or at least what was left of it. Everything was blackened and partly melted.

"It's not too late," I said.

"Too late for what?" Ratchet said. "What does all this mean?"

"The Urgos is the clock Fuzee used to represent. When it was damaged and replaced, she lost the ability to move between worlds. She used to be a spandrel, like us. She wants to leave, I just know it. Fixing the Urgos will give her the chance."

"But we don't have the parts for an Urgos," Adele said. "It's one of a kind."

"Not exactly," Ratchet said with the snap of his fingers. "The Hoffhalder is nearly identical. They were built in the same German village."

"I'll get it," Adele said. She hopped off the counter and exited the room. Ratchet followed right behind her.

"Bring it to Albert's workshop—I mean, my workshop." Fortunately, the Urgos box had handles on it. I lifted it and held it close to my stomach as I walked it out of the room. Last time I was here I took the elevator to the workshop, but I knew there was a small staircase that led directly to it. The wooden stairs creaked as the Urgos and I carefully made our way down. The others were right behind me.

The workshop was empty when we entered, but I expected

that. I put the box down and made a circular motion with my finger. The lights came on, and all the clocks suddenly appeared, pendulums swinging in time. The main workbench was directly ahead of me, but I didn't need it. The space in the middle of the floor would do just fine.

"Place the Hoffhalder over there," I said, pointing to a spot on the floor to my right.

Ratchet had already taken the Urgos and its various pieces out and placed them directly in front of me. An image appeared in my head of what I wanted to accomplish. I could see the finished movement turning and ticking away. Now it was time to make it happen.

I summoned a small tool from the workbench and removed the back of the Hoffhalder with ease. Then the parts started flying. I took as many as I could from the Hoffhalder and attached them to the Urgos. The center post, the intermediate wheel, and much of the chime train were salvageable from the Urgos, although badly charred. Many of the items just needed cleaning, so I called for some solvent and the small tools required for the job. Then came the most important part: the mainspring. The Hoffhalder was a smaller clock with a slightly smaller movement than the Urgos, but the mainspring was nearly the same size. I carefully lifted it from one clock to the other and secured it.

"Good job," Ratchet said. "I think it may just work."

"Let's find out," I said. I took a key and wound the Urgos ever so slightly. The gears and pinions began to do their thing. It worked! I moved the hands to the top of the hour, and it gave out a low chime.

"So now what?" Adele asked. "How will you get this Fuzee person to come back with you?"

I wasn't entirely sure, but I didn't want the others to know that. "First I have to put the Urgos back in its station. The path to it is still around, but I'll bet it hasn't been used in a long time. After that, I'll just have to charm her."

Ratchet was whispering something to Adele, who looked at me, then nodded. They seemed quite concerned but made no attempt to share. It didn't matter, because I had things to do.

"Let me just clean up first." The tools, unused parts, cleaning supplies, and other items flew into their bins and drawers.

"Are you sure you want to do this?" Ratchet asked. "I've never heard of it working before."

"I'm sure. Are you going to wish me luck or what?"

He put his hand on my shoulder. "Good luck and be careful. Do you need our help?"

"No thanks. I'll take it from here." I made a pushing

motion with my right hand. "You may want to back up a bit."

Next was the isochronal circle. Timepieces flew off the walls and out of drawers and soon began circling just in front of me. I summoned a cage from the corner of the room and placed the Urgos inside it. It was time to leave.

"This is a wonderful thing you're doing," Adele said.

"I love ya, you little pip," Ratchet added.

I picked up the Urgos and stepped into the circle.

CHAPTER TWENTY-TWO

Things were different in Furtwangen. I arrived in the Sequence, and it was much brighter than before. Gone were most of the mist and fog and other mysterious elements I was used to seeing. The catwalk remained, thankfully, and I had no time to waste getting to my destination. I passed a large clock on my right, Ripley Park, which told me I was only two clocks away from the three o'clock position. There were no gearheads, just an occasional worker getting to his or her clock station. I ran as fast as I could along the metal path until it veered just slightly to the right. This is where they'd had to adjust the path to a new clock when the Urgos was taken off-line many decades ago. I passed the new clock, and it was being worked on by several workers. It was "life goes on" here in Kinzig.

Just up ahead, I came to the old path that led to the Urgos. I was wrong about the fog and mist being gone. It had all accumulated here, or so it seemed. I jumped the rail and took my cage along toward the Urgos, determined not to let the mist and fog stop me. I could see the clock tower just ahead of me, but there was nothing there but a small black box. That's all it took to run the digital clock that replaced the Urgos.

I placed the cage down and disconnected a cable running into the black box, killing the digital display. Somebody down below may notice, but I didn't care. I wouldn't be long. I took out the Urgos movement and placed it on top of the black box. No one on the outside would see the Urgos because it was mostly just the guts. I wound the Urgos, and the gears began to move.

All I could do was wait and hope.

It seemed like minutes, but it was probably just a few seconds—it was hard to tell in the mist—before Fuzee arrived. She walked slowly toward me while looking down at the clock in front of me.

"The Urgos," she said. "You-you fixed it."

"You are fully represented again. I used some parts from the Hoffhalder to make it happen."

She reached down and touched the Urgos movement,

some of it still blackened. "Why did you do this?"

"Come back with me, Fuzee. You can now. Come live on the other side."

She looked at me with those huge eyes and gave me a big hug. "You shouldn't have done this for me. I don't know—"

"We have to move quickly, while the isochronal circle is still active." I grabbed her shoulders. "Please."

Her head shook as her eyes spun around. She was certainly thinking about it. Finally, the shake turned into a nod. "Okay. Let's go."

This time I took her hand and led. We dashed along the path through the mist until we came to the catwalk rail, which we easily scaled.

"This way," I said, heading back toward the Ripley Park clock. I sneaked a peek back at Fuzee, and she had the biggest smile I had ever seen. Good thing no one else was on the path because we weren't stopping for anything.

We reached the arrival spot and huddled together. When she took my hand, I knew something was wonderfully different. Fuzee was no longer a clock part. She was a real girl. The prettiest girl I had ever seen.

"Fuzee, you're—"

She put her hands on my shoulders and pulled me toward her. This time I didn't resist my first-ever kiss. We both enjoyed the moment with eyes wide open, and none of them were spinning. A little fog rolled in, and the sparkles from the circle filled the area around us. She pulled away just as we arrived back in the clock shop. Superb!

We stepped out of the circle and were greeted by Ratchet and Adele.

"She's beautiful," Adele said.

I led her over to a full-length mirror behind the door. Gone was the cone-shaped body she'd morphed into over the years in Furtwangen. Her shoulders were large, and the rest of her lean. Her old-fashioned dress went just below her knees. She still had curly brown hair, but her eyes were a normal size—okay, maybe a bit bigger than normal—but still awesome.

"Welcome to the other side," I said, as she continued to look at herself in the mirror.

"Suzie," she said. "I remember now. I used to be known as Suzie. There is so much I've missed. I don't know where to start."

The isochronal circle still swirled in the corner. Soon it was filled with modern images. "We have cars and skyscrapers, and flat-screen TVs and computers." The images popped in and out of the circle. "There's lots to see in this world."

She watched for a while, and then turned away dejectedly.

"This isn't my time."

"I know it's not. I'll help you figure it out. It'll be fun."

She turned away from the circle and the mass of images. My plan was not working at all.

Ratchet stepped forward and made some adjustments to the circle. "Maybe this will help, Suzie."

The images we were from many years ago, perhaps the early 1900s. The people wore old-fashioned clothes, like Fuzee—I mean, Suzie—was wearing. People moved around in carriages, and the women carried small umbrellas over their shoulders. Suzie's eyes lit up. "This is my time. This is where I'd like to go."

"But-but, we won't be together. I thought you wanted to be with me."

"I would like that more than anything. I really would. But I can't live in your world. I'm sorry."

Adele put her hand on my shoulder. "Let her go." Ratchet nodded in agreement.

I stepped back from the circle and motioned Suzie into it. A huge lump formed in my throat, and I was glad I didn't have to talk right then.

There was no theatrical goodbye kiss or anything like that. She simply smiled that wonderful smile and walked into the circle. Just like that, she was gone. Back to her time.

Ratchet took me by the shoulders and pulled me away. The images of her time continued to display as I backed up. She was gone, and I would never see her again. This was not how it was supposed to play out. We were supposed to end up together.

"I know it's hard to give up something you love," Ratchet said. "But Adele and I were discussing the ramifications of what happened. By using the clock you represent to fix the Urgos, you would have lost your powers. If she stayed here, you would not be the Tick Tock Man. I think this worked out for the best."

I would have given up my powers in a second to have her back. I didn't care about the stupid clock-making skills. I wanted to be with Suzie.

"I think it's time to go home," Ratchet said. "Your parents are worried about you. Look."

The isochronal circle still flashed images of them talking in the dining room. They were near where the Hoffhalder used to be. Then the talk turned to an argument. I couldn't hear him, but I knew Dad was pretty ticked off. His precious clock was gone and never coming back. I would be grounded until, well, probably until I was fourteen. Maybe I could just live in the shop. Oh yeah. How would I explain that?

New images began to fill the circle. There were more

scenes of long ago, back in Suzie's time. Then Suzie's face appeared, and she smiled. She reached out her hand.

A sudden surge of energy filled me. I realized Ratchet and Adele were not completely truthful about me losing my power. They were just trying to protect me.

I am the Tick Tock Man. I have the power to go wherever I want, whenever I want.

I took a step toward Suzie.

"Carlton, no!" Ratchet yelled. "Don't do it, you little pip!" He tried to grab me, but he missed.

"I'll come back, I swear." I jumped into the circle.

THE END

ACKNOWLEDGEMENTS

I would like to thank the wonderful folks at Month9 Publishing for their tireless work on this book. Thanks to editors Tara Creel and Jana Armstrong, proofreader Barbara VanDenburgh, cover designer Danielle Doolittle, author liaison Jennifer Million and publisher Georgia McBride, who saw something wonderful in this manuscript and gave it a home. Kudos to my front line and beta readers Kelly Andrews, Ellyn Ritterskamp, Nancy Christy, Roland Lacroix and Kim Cogburn. Thanks for making the words better. Much gratitude to my internet friends the BBs, YNots and Purgies who make life online bearable. Keep up the good work. Warm hugs to my family for their never-ending support and understanding.

R. M. CLARK

R. M. Clark is a scientist for the Dept. of Navy by day and children's book writer by night. He lives in Massachusetts with his wife and two sons. He is currently at work on his latest middle grade novel.

Visit his author site: www.rmclarkauthor.com

OTHER MONTH9BOOKS TITLES YOU MIGHT LIKE

THE MAGNIFICENT GLASS GLOBE
JOSHUA AND THE LIGHTNING ROAD

Find more books like this at:
http://www.Month9Books.com

Connect with Month9Books online:
Facebook: www.Facebook.com/Month9Books
Twitter: https://twitter.com/Month9Books
You Tube: www.youtube.com/user/Month9Books
Tumblr: http://month9books.tumblr.com/
Instagram: https://instagram.com/month9books

AN OLD CHEST. A TRANSLUCENT GLOBE. A MAGICAL ADVENTURE BEYOND THEIR WILDEST DREAMS.

THE MAGNIFICENT GLASS GLOBE

N. R. BERGESON

JOSHUA
AND THE
LIGHTNING
ROAD

DONNA GALANTI

THE TICK TOCK MAN

R.M. CLARK

THE TICK TOCK MAN by R.M. Clark
All rights reserved. Published in the United States of America by Month9Books, LLC.
No part of this book may be used or reproduced in any manner whatsoever without written permission of the publisher, except in the case of brief quotations embodied in critical articles and reviews.

Trade Paperback ISBN: 978-1-944816-60-5
ePub ISBN: 978-1-946700-03-2
Mobipocket ISBN: 978-1-946700-04-9

Published by Tantrum Books for Month9Books, Raleigh, NC 27609
Cover design by Danielle Doolittle

To my mother, Jan. The time is right.